THIS IS
NOT
WHERE IT
ENDS

THIS IS NOT WHERE IT ENDS

a novel

RICHARD ALAN CARTER

ARCHWAY
PUBLISHING

Archway Publishing books may be ordered
through booksellers or by contacting:

Archway Publishing
1663 Liberty Drive
Bloomington, IN 47403
www.archwaypublishing.com
1 (888) 242-5904

Because of the dynamic nature of the Internet, any web addresses or
links contained in this book may have changed since publication and
may no longer be valid. The views expressed in this work are solely those
of the author and do not necessarily reflect the views of the publisher,
and the publisher hereby disclaims any responsibility for them.

Cover photo credit: John Rennison, at *The Hamilton Spectator.*

ISBN: 978-1-4808-1967-2 (sc)
ISBN: 978-1-4808-1968-9 (hc)
ISBN: 978-1-4808-1969-6 (e)

Library of Congress Control Number: 2015946809

Print information available on the last page.

Archway Publishing rev. date: 8/4/2015

For Gisele,
who brought her own light

She closed the door behind her, pulled the drapes shut, took off her shoes, stood on a chair, popped out the battery from the smoke detector, sat down on the edge of the bed, and lit a cigarette. The drone from the cars outside on the highway mixed with the fan tumbling around in the room's air-conditioning unit; a brown-tinged white noise washed over her. She closed her eyes and exhaled. The air in the motel was heavy, cool, and musty. She sat there as if underwater and allowed her mind to clear—her thoughts floating away, dissipating.

She kept her eyes closed as she smoked, the ash wafting across her legs and onto the carpeting. *How long has it been?* she wondered. How long had it been since the last time she'd stopped running around worrying about every little thing? Stopped worrying what everyone else thought and if they were okay?

How long, huh? Never, maybe?

It sure as hell seemed like maybe never.

Footsteps and muffled speech on the other side of the door brought her back to the present. Her eyes blinked open just in time to see someone pass in front of the window. She got up and walked into the bathroom, dropping the cigarette butt into the toilet before dropping herself onto the seat. Leaning forward with her head nearly between her knees, she peed hard. Out, that's what she wanted. She wanted it out. But that wasn't going to happen was it?

Silly girl, she thought. *You got just what you wanted. You always got just what you wanted. You got your husband and your kid, your house in the suburbs, and a job that you don't need. But at least that job gives you a sense of identity, right? Especially here in a town full of people who care more about what they do for a living than what kind of a person they are. You got everything you wanted, and now what?*

"Now what, goddamn it?" she yelled, standing up in one quick, fluid motion. Turning, she reached out and flushed. "Now what?" she mouthed silently as she watched the butt circle the bowl and drop out of sight.

She walked back into the bedroom and sought out the clock; *twelve forty-five, everyone's still at lunch.* It'd be another hour before anyone at her job began to wonder where she was. She had time, and she had a decision to make. *I could use a drink.* But this wasn't the kind of place with a minibar tucked into the closet. This was the kind of place where the occupants brought their own. Looking around the room, her guess was that there'd been lots of them with lots of it. Climbing onto the bed, she pushed aside the pillow and lay flat on her back.

The Silly Girl Who Always Got What She Wanted

Oh man, how long ago had it been since that fairy tale got wiped?

Little princesses dream big (if not particularly original) dreams. And hey, if you grew up in some redneck shithole, you wouldn't mock the escape value of a good fairy tale. It's a fine line that separates a girl from the leering, tattooed masses of inhumanity and the cold, manufactured sheen of vinyl double-paned insularity. You may have played with your Barbie in a trailer, but your Barbie didn't live in one. How many lithe young millworkers' daughters jumped on the first bankroll to come their way? Years later, they all ended up the same, though: broken by the sight of themselves wearing a tablecloth and bent over spanking some screaming kid in the aisle of Shopper's Food Warehouse.

It's funny now to think about how much she thought she hated that place. In retrospect, it was nothing more than boredom and a sense of adventure that put her in the arms of a boy who would provide a ticket to somewhere else— wherever the hell that was. Growing up, she lived there, and that was that. It was only later, when her father was ill—dying on a bed they'd set up in the front room of the house he'd spent a lifetime sweating blood for and raising a family in—that she came to see it for what it was.

She saw the rotted wood flooring in all corners of the kitchen, the lopsided screen doors, and the sagging drywall ceilings. All those streets with no sidewalks, covered in soot-streaked snow under a gray sky, lined with one stagnant pile of lives after another. She was out front smoking, and she saw a dog across the street chained to a post, in the way only someone without pretense could have done. The poor creature was straining toward a fixed point in the distance. *But aren't we all?* she mused wryly. She watched as it circled and pulled, backed up and circled again. The struggle within manifested in a futility of effort transfixed. And for a moment she wanted to release the hero, see him break free and run—all the way back to the land of plenty, to bite the first one of her pretentious neighbors who tottered out onto their sculpted lawn.

Pricks

When her daddy died, a door closed on something she never saw coming. Her past came into focus without the distance of hindsight. For the first time in her life, she was at home. In a place she hadn't lived for nearly thirty years, her heart finally exhaled.

In the house, in the ambulance, in the hospital.

In the casket, in the church, in the ground.

In the end, it all seemed like a beginning, one from which she was now going to turn her back. It was time to just walk away.

With everyone looking on, she cried. She cried for her dead father, who'd spent his final years alone in the house, his days culminating as he quietly and politely turned down one anonymous phone solicitation after another. She cried because her own time was speeding up. She cried because she was only now making the effort and putting in the emotional capital to follow up on the life she'd long ago surrendered to the easy group-think construction of quintessential middle-class nonsense.

She sat up.

The room grew darker, and the traffic outside sounded fuller. Standing, she smoothed down her blouse with both hands while making eye contact with herself in the mirror across the room. She was cool and dry as she slowly made her way closer to the reflection. Pulling the clothing over and off with one hand, she stopped to peer directly into her own face. That morning in the shower, she'd been enveloped by tears. It was raining tears all around her, and she had been … what? Scared? Confused? Something. Her compass had spun under the fixture. She pressed her hand flat against her belly and slid it up and under her breast. She let her fingers press ever so lightly and rest on the lump. Her nose tingled, she watched the single tear develop, and she knew.

On the evening of his forty-ninth birthday, the policeman walked out to his cruiser, as he had nearly every evening for twenty-five years. He stood and read the motto embossed on the door panel before getting in:

"To Protect and Serve"

People say they are not defined by what they do for a living, yet no such thought crossed Officer Nelson Little's mind. He buckled up, turned the ignition, put the air-conditioning on low, radioed in to the dispatcher, and pulled out onto the road. Another night of service in the town of dwindling means commenced.

He moved steadily through what little traffic there was. More often than not, the others cars yielded the right-of-way once they realized a police presence. Slowly gliding along, he scanned the pedestrians making their way along the sidewalks. He noted passenger-seat occupants eyeing him. He saw someone letting their dog relieve itself next to a mailbox. He watched a man's hat as it blew off his head in the aftermath of a passing truck and sailed out into traffic, the owner cursing its arc. Someone reached out of a bus stop shelter and gave him the finger.

* * *

The town itself was a hodgepodge of all things old and older. Today's crumbling concrete strip malls erected uneasily alongside the long-ago abandoned industrial blocks of yesterday; rooted elderly matrons gave no quarter to the sharp elbows of indifferent usurpers.

Forty-nine years ago, he'd been born in this town, the only child of a local son turned truck driver and a Midwest farm girl graduated to town life, looking for work. Back then, it had been a collection of small, working-class neighborhoods on what a generation before had been farmland. Every once in a while, he'd hear someone talking on the local news about how much better it had been then, or he'd see an old picture in the paper of a long-gone street corner—and he'd *almost* buy into it.

And then he'd remember the glare to his happy life under the sun.

He thought of a Confederate flag, purposely set out in front of some house, waving in ill-tempered defiance for all with eyes to see.

He thought of those overseas boat kids showing up as a group one day, like children from another planet, being led into his classroom. He thought of how they were set upon by the jeering offspring of those who'd not learned before them.

He thought of the retarded kid down the street who'd gone to the bathroom in his pants. That boy laughed with the crowd surrounding him, his eyes filled with tears. You could all but hear the screaming inside if you tried.

As the years went by, those memories and the associated guilt they were soaked in fueled a desire to do something more than it had taken to get that far: the default position of one who had not stood out. He'd observed some bad things happen, as most kids will eventually, but never took the taint of actual action with him. And while he knew pretty much everyone in his neighborhood, when they all up and moved out piecemeal for the big cities and the money they implied, he realized later that he'd been alone the whole time without even noticing.

His mother was the thinker, the one who'd wanted more for her only child. To have made it this far for her had been a real achievement. To see her son remain static in a place where she had taken a step forward was something that he later suspected she'd resigned herself to. In the last few years, as she receded into illness, confined to a wheelchair, confined to their house, he'd taken to telling her about his work, in part because she loved to hear what was going on outside of her four walls, and to impart some sense of what his work meant to him, that he wasn't just biding time in his life. Officer Nelson Little came to realize that it didn't take much of an investigation to find out that this girl in glasses from the cold northern acres had learned to make do with less than she deserved, silently watching her dreams slip away.

So his job took on a role in his mind that he dared not mention—a cleansing redemption, a chance to steady the tilting lives that surrounded him in unstable situations. He was a solid presence in a familiar environment looking for an opportunity to intervene. Alone among a division of armed men empowered to exert the enforcement of law, he saw past action and on into motivation. He had seen the idealism of the newly indoctrinated crush lightly under the weight of the seasoned cynic. He became, he needed to be, a stalwart against the swinging truncheons of the disillusioned majority.

In other words Officer Nelson Little was inherently incapable of escaping his unerring sense of right and wrong—much to the dismay of several coworkers. They who were nothing more than small-town bullies given a chance to act out with the full force of the law behind them. As such, Officer Little was as likely to follow up station calls that required climbing trees for errant pets and retirement home residential arguments as he was to assist in the resolution of any actual criminal activity. He never saw this as anything other than his duty as a policeman. As a result, he was mocked ruthlessly. He took this as good-natured ribbing between men with tough jobs; they hated his guts for not being able to openly flaunt their graft.

*　*　*

"9-1 this is Dispatch," his radio buzzed. "Little, you out there?"

He'd gotten the call. There was a disturbance at the new Chuck E Cheese restaurant on the edge of town; go and see what it was all about. He tightened his seat belt, flipped on the strobe light, and let the sirens scream. "This," he told himself, "is what it's all about."

Arriving on the scene, Officer Nelson Little stepped out into what would be one of the defining moments of his life. "My god ...," he mouthed, exiting his cruiser into what looked to him to be something akin to an apocalypse.

The parking lot was full of screaming children running amuck in every direction, parents screaming and running after them. The noise was deafening. The ground was littered with party hats, and the sky was full of balloon clusters. A man in a giant mouse costume was lying face down just outside the entrance. A torn sack leaking money in small denominations was next to him, the bills blowing out over the lot like green confetti.

"What on earth is going on here?" He turned around slowly and surveyed the scene.

A small girl was in front of him, alone, holding a balloon in one hand and a leash in the other. The dog had a bow on its head and was yelping incessantly; the girl was wearing a pointed party hat and screaming.

"It's going to be all right, honey," he said, kneeling down to look her in the face.

She stopped screaming, and he saw her eyes widen, registering something behind him.

He stood back up and turned around.

The giant mouse was back on its feet, the money bag clutched in one hand and a gun pointing out of the other.

And the bottom fell out.

Officer Nelson Little had just enough time to raise his left hand up, palm out flat toward the giant mouse, when the air around his presence shuddered into an explosion.

His arm went numb to the shoulder, a thundering roar built in his ears, and his hand disappeared in a splash.

He saw his ring finger pinwheel out of the blur and spin up into the air.

He stumbled around, stepped off the curb, and fell over back-ward onto the asphalt.

His heart was beating.

He could see the girl was still there.

She raised her hands to her mouth in a scream he couldn't hear.

The dog scooped up his finger in its mouth and ran off into the melee.

And on this day—this day of all days—looking up, his eyes lost focus on the "Happy Birthday!" balloon as both he and it floated away.

The baby sat there and frowned at her across the waiting room, squirming and fidgeting as if trying to worm its way out of her line of sight. The mother, without taking her nose out of a well-thumbed magazine she was leaning into, reached back and without looking pushed the baby back into position next to her. For a moment the two of them sat still, until the baby looked across the room again and resumed telegraphing its apparent dissatisfaction.

Yeah, me too, she thought.

Was this a mistake? Was she jumping to conclusions?

"Clara Kozlowski?"

Startled, the baby began to cry. Somewhere deep in the walls the air-conditioning clicked on, and the environment began to circulate.

She stood up and walked toward the nurse in the doorway, following her into and down the hallway beyond. The nurse stopped at a door, opened it, and motioned for her to enter.

"Here you go, dear. Take everything off from the waist up and put this on, the opening in the front." Placing her hand flat on a green paper gown spread out on the table, she continued, "The doctor will be with you in a moment."

Looking up at Clara, having bent forward to smooth a paper cover across the examination table, her warm eyes wavered, and she silently stepped backward out of the room, pulling the door shut behind her.

The air-conditioning brought a distant sobbing from elsewhere lightly through the vent and into the room. Clara slipped out of her top dressings and carefully folded them into a neat triangle, setting them down on one of the stools under which she'd placed her shoes. Wrapped in paper, she hoisted herself up onto the examination table and, with the cool metal edge nestled behind her knees, closed her eyes and waited.

*   *   *

"There is a lump," the doctor was saying.

Clara's stomach clenched. Something inside her began to fall, descending, and her ears picked up the movement of a clock on the wall. "Oh god, no … no," fingers trembling, and the hairs on her head prickled.

He lowered his voice. "I'm being straight with you, Clara." He held up both hands as if braking any thoughts from going further. "There are no foregone conclusions. Lumpy breasts? I've been a doctor since you were just a little girl, and I've seen nearly every conceivable variation of this diagnosis. Caffeine, caffeine, of all things, can, believe it or not, cause women to develop a lump on their breast. That alone suggests the endless possibilities of what we are dealing with here."

And her mother was holding her, slowly combing her fingers through Clara's hair and telling her that she, " ... could do anything you put your mind to. Honey, you only have to try, and it will happen."

"But," pulling his glasses off, looking directly at Clara now, "this is something that could be nothing. We want to be sure. You want to be sure. We'll schedule you for a mammogram and a biopsy, and that will point conclusively one way or the other."

And her daddy had her hand in his, standing so tall beside her, together looking up at stars sprayed across the night sky, telling her that, " ... the possibilities are endless. Like a dream that you will grow up in and make your own."

"We fight, Clara, you and I and everyone here. Together." The doctor sat down on a stool at the end of the examination table. "Life ...," he suddenly looked his age, "all life, your life, is worth the fight. And that," he smiled softly at her, "is my professional opinion."

And her sister is there with her, under a blanket pulled over their heads, in bed and warm against the cold dark—their fingers interlocked and promising each other, " ... to always be there together. Forever."

She looked away and lost the doctor's voice. On the other side of a small high window, a tiny red bird was warbling frantically, muffled behind the glass, head bobbing quickly to and fro, accentuating its busy chorus, looking at her.

Why, Clara mouthed in response. The bird flew away.

"Do you have any questions, Clara?"

"Just one," looking up through tears into the old doctor's perception.

"Yes, of course," smiling at her directness. "There really is only the one, isn't there?" He stood up slowly, supporting himself with a hand on the table next to where she was sitting. "You can get dressed now. Schedule that procedure, Clara. Don't think it over; just do it. Get yourself ready and get back to us. Soon."

He held her hand in his for a moment before opening the door and walking out.

Her first instinct was to rush after him, shouting questions she hadn't even fully formulated yet, anything to not let it go just yet. Instead she pulled over the stool and shook out her clothes before getting dressed. Once she had her shoes on, she bent underneath the small faucet along the wall and let the water run across her face and into her mouth. She walked coolly out of the room, hurried down the hall past the receptionist, who had only a moment to just slightly acknowledge her presence, and was practically running when she reached the front doors. Coming fast out into an atmosphere of oppressive heat, she slid on top of the crumbling concrete sidewalk, nearly lost her footing, and in balancing herself, threw her arms out and loudly gasped for breath.

Without thinking, oblivious to several startled onlookers, Clara Kozlowski ran as fast and as hard as she could across the parking lot.

*　*　*

Pulling the stale pie-crust-like cookie apart with her fingers, Clara let it crumble and fall to the table in pieces. Carefully, with both hands, she smoothed out the oily paper rectangle to read the fortune,

And found a blank strip of paper.

Ensconced at The Lucky Duck Dine-In-Take-Out and enveloped in the late-afternoon light of a front window booth, ignoring the coffee she'd ordered but not drunk and having pulled the cellophane-wrapped cookie from a plastic basket on the table, she smiled to herself and turned the nonfortune around several times in her fingers.

Really? she thought, beginning to wind down.

On the street outside, the rush hour was getting under way. The pace of life was quickening. Everywhere she looked, faces on the other side of the glass seemed to reflect an internal conduit between where they had been and what lay ahead. A daily cycle of obligation and concern brought to a close, a seemingly ubiquitous sense of relief.

Clara wondered when it would be before she felt that way again.

"You no eat cookie?"

Clara turned to see the proprietress frowning at the small pile of jagged crumbs on the table in front of her. Holding out the fortune before folding it and putting it into her purse, she smiled and said, "No, but this I like."

Drawing her finger around in the crumb pile, she looked into the older woman's skeptical face. A smile was hiding there somewhere.

A cloud sailed across the sunset, and its shadow suddenly cooled her as it floated past. She felt calm standing there at the crosswalk. A small red bird was standing on the lamppost busily cheeping at her from overhead.

"Hey you!" she yelled up.

Unmindful of her surroundings, thinking of her nonfortune and the undetermined future it implied; this was the first time all day she'd been okay with not having an answer.

You mean to tell me that you found a lump, and you're just now getting around to telling me about it?"

He sounded incredulous. She stared at him seated in front of the computer, remaining seated in front of the computer.

"I mean, when did it occur to you that *maybe* you should tell your husband, for God's sake?" He furrowed his brow and shook his head. She caught him glimpse at the screen.

"Jesus, Clara, we are up to our neck in it—the mortgage, the kid's school. Hell, the list goes on! You know this." He stared at the monitor. "If you're sick, then we really have to consider what we're going to do here, you know? I already work day in and day out. I don't know what you expect me to do."

I work too, she thought.

"I just needed to think. To get my mind around it first, see how I felt."

"See how you felt?" He rested both his hands on the keyboard. "Did you stop to think about how I would feel, huh?" He was drumming his fingers. "It's *us* here, Clara—you and me. Whatever is going on with you is going on with me. Your responsibilities are my responsibilities. Christ almighty, what am I supposed to do now?"

He sat staring at the computer. She stood staring at him.

*   *   *

He'd been something else entirely when she first met him.

Growing up, those boys in her hometown had been rough-edged kids raised by tougher parents. She'd held out longer than most, before finally she heard what many before her had been attuned to: "You're young and pretty, you're going nowhere, and life is short and ugly. What are you waiting for? Get in there."

And she did.

Or rather, she'd started to, started to want to, when "something else" made his first appearance.

There was a template to life there that was if not expected, then certainly used with no one second-guessing your decision: finish school, take a shift in the mills or apron-up in the diners lining the roads home, hook up, get married, move in with someone's folks, have kids, save your money and buy a house, hopefully not too close to someone's folks and settle down for the long haul. Like someone's folks before you. All told it wasn't a bad life. No matter what was happening off one of those faraway interstate exits that ran past outside of town, if you were here, you were more than just home. You were a part of everything that was home to everyone here. You were safe.

But here was someone who was comparatively different. Not necessarily better, just … different. Maybe just enough?

On the town bus sitting directly across from him, everything known rushing past in the windows, she sat there quietly looking forward. Community college boy? That was an unknown without priors. He sat there and looked back at her: big hair, short skirt, bigger dreams. On his way out the door, would there be one last option?

Here we go, she thought.

And eventually they did go. She took his hand and his offer and some cosmetology classes, and then the offer he made after that and everything that followed: the ring, the marriage, the move far away, the house, the family.

Except for her name, her daddy's name, she took it all.

*   *   *

And it had all led to what? She lay on her side of the bed and thought this over for the umpteenth time. It wasn't as if she had any solid, concrete grounds to complain on. It was more like a slow accumulation of small slights that over time had begun to color the whole picture.

That, *and acting like a dick.*

She turned and looked at the lighted dial: nearly two in the morning. She sat up and looked to the other, vacant, side of the bed. Apparently Mister Work-from-home-information-technology was still at it. Saving today's businessman from himself, one porn-riddled p.c. workstation after another.

She got out of the bed and into her slippers. She grabbed the pack of cigarettes and the lighter off the dresser, dropped them into her gown's pocket, and quietly padded her way down the stairs. She could hear the faint tapping of intermittent keystrokes coming from behind the closed home office door. She stood there and listened for a minute before moving through the kitchen and silently opening the back door, buffering the lock with her hand as she pulled it partially closed behind her.

It was still muggy out but cooler. There wasn't a cloud in the sky. She lit a cigarette, tipped her head back, and slowly blew the smoke up in a thin plume. She felt better now than she had all of the previous day. She kicked off her slippers and set her feet down into the moist grass. She could smell the earth. She closed her eyes and listened as the sound of a passing car evaporated into the distance.

She walked around to the side of the house, the computer inside casting a neon blue glow out of a downstairs window. She stubbed out her cigarette in the sodden turf and then quietly pushed herself between the bushes and up to the window.

She peeked in.

He was there in front of his computer, as usual. She squinted and looked closely.

What was he doing in there all night? she thought to herself.

She was nearly pressing her face against the glass now. He was sitting down and leaning forward, his chest nearly touching the table edge. His face staring directly at the monitor screen, his pajama pants pulled down around his knees, he was furiously masturbating under the table into one of her good guest towels.

You have got to be kidding me! she nearly blurted out.

She pushed her way back out of the bushes and stood there in the yard. "Well, that about does it," she said aloud to herself. There were a lot of things she needed to get straight in her life right now, but two very specific answers, to two very specific questions, came to her right there and then:

She was going to need to get away from here before she would be able to work through the last couple of days.

And that selfish son of a bitch can do his own damn laundry this week.

It was the smell of burning hair that snapped her out of it. She peeked at the client's reflection in the mirror, eyes still closed, as she seamlessly rolled out the curling iron and smoothed down the crinkled follicles with a wet comb.

"Just a few more minutes, Mrs. D. Are you doing okay?"

The elderly client looked up, eyes blinking like some newly hatched blue-haired baby bird. "Oh yes, dear," she croaked hoarsely, clearing her throat. "You take your time." She smiled at her in the mirror before closing her eyes again.

Clara grabbed the scissors and quickly clipped off the crystallized tips, then ran the blow dryer for a minute to clear the air while resuming the curling. She pulled a nonchalant assessment of the shop, before turning back to the task at hand.

Like most Fridays, it had been a full morning. She was glad when she saw the sign on the door turn over signaling the noon break. So, until one-thirty when she'd have to be back to set up for the two o'clock appointments, her time was her own. She grabbed her purse, folded the morning's tips into her name-monogrammed smock pocket, popped on her tortoise-shell sunglasses and stepped out the back door into the sun. She took a couple of deep breaths to clear out the scent of nail polish remover and perm-paste before digging out a cigarette and lighting it, walking over to the employee picnic table, and sitting down in the shade.

A long four-door sedan rolled into the parking lot and made a slow U-turn, pulling up to the curb in front of her. "Hey, Clara," waved the driver through the open passenger side window. "Queenie on her way out, did ya notice?"

"Hi, Billy," she said. "She's probably washing up. One of those last-minute Weekend Special walk-ins, you know?"

"Oh yeah, great," he glazed over. "Guess we'll have something to talk about over lunch then, huh?"

As the door opened, and Queenie stepped out, copper skin glowing in the light, sky-blue sun dress billowing in the wind, red bandana corseting the towering pile of hair, she radiated ease.

Clara looked her up and down as she approached. "How do you do it?"

"It's all in the pre-sen-ta-tion, baby," she said, slapping herself on the butt. "Hey, honey," leaning down and looking Clara straight on, "You okay, huh? You seem a little, I dunno, dis-tracted maybe? Hmm? Is everything all right?"

"I'm fine." Clara took notice: real concern. "Just tired."

"Yeah, okay," Queenie nodded. "Hey, look, why don't you come with Billy and me, huh? He's taking me over to the Double RR for lunch, and maybe we could sneak a couple of drinks in before we have to be back, you know, just because we deserve it, yeah?"

"That's nice, thanks. But I think I'm just going to sit here for a bit, maybe take a walk. Get some air." She looked over her sunglasses and smiled.

"Well, okay. But If I don't show up at two, you'll know you missed out," and she winked. "Hey, look, baby, you take it easy, all right, and I'll see you in a couple of hours," and she ran her palm across Clara's cheek before heading off to the car with a wave bye.

Clara waved back, watching her go before taking one last drag on the cigarette and then flicking it, not seeing it bounce off the lip of the sand pail. She sat and watched the guys at the car wash across the street busily wiping down one vehicle after another as they slowly rolled out from under the brushes and blowers. An indistinct sound of voices, mixed with the occasional laugh, was carrying across the road. Not a care in the world.

There are no foregone conclusions.

She could hear the doctor's voice echoing in her head as she watched the guys across the street. *All life, your life, is worth the fight.* She suddenly felt sick to her stomach. She stood up and walked out to the sidewalk. There was a light breeze. She hesitated for a moment and then turned and started walking headlong into the moving air, letting it cool her face and legs as she moved along.

My life, she thought.

Why on earth wasn't she at the hospital right now? Was it that she couldn't be sure her life, unlike an illness, possibly a disease, as it was, could be saved? How about not being so pretentious, she told herself.

And yet ... what?

"My life," she considered out loud, and quickly rolled her head around.

She thought of her sister back in their hometown, whom she spent all of her childhood looking up to. They could now barely find the time to send each other a card on holidays. She thought of her son and wondered how often he thought of her. She thought of her husband, the man she had vowed to spend her life with, and wondered if he still felt the same way? When was the last time he'd said that he loved her? She couldn't remember. She also couldn't remember the last time she'd told him either. What were they doing to each other, what were they doing to their lives, in their lives?

"Whaaaaaaaaaaaaaaaaaaaaaaaaoooooooooooooo!"

A car slowed enough for her to see the thick-necked guy in the football jersey toss out the side window, and hit her with, an empty fountain-drink cup. A bit of backwash spotted her top as it bounced off her chest and fell into the gutter. "Damn!" she exclaimed, dropping her head and stepping back with one foot.

She just stood there for a minute breathing heavily, hearing the car's passenger laughing as it swerved off down the road. Taking a tissue out of her purse and licking it first lightly, she daubed at the speckle. Looking up, a diner-style family restaurant was about a block farther up the road. She drew in a mouth-full of air, regained her composure, and made her way over.

* * *

Pushing open the glass door, the air-conditioning washed over her as she stepped into the dimmer atmosphere—one-level dining room with booths and wood paneling, one side lined with a lunch counter. Hot plates sat on a sill from the kitchen for table delivery. There couldn't have been more than a handful of customers in the whole place. She spotted the restrooms and made her way over.

Inside, she wet a towel and, as best she could, scrubbed out the pink syrup from her top. She had a Taser in her purse, one of those that you see on home shopping shows. She'd never taken it out even once since buying it. She thought about how it would feel to be lighting up that quarterback's nuts right now and smiled to herself.

Eventually sitting down at the counter, she pulled out her cigarettes and lighter and immediately heard, "Not in here, sweetie." A waitress strolled over, chomping gum and pushing a pencil in and out behind her ear. "The next thing you know they'll start telling you what you can and can't eat, and then I guess they'll have to shut this place down." She showed Clara her crooked front teeth and then leaned down onto the counter in front of her. "What can I get for you?"

"Coffee, please." She looked around at the glass case sitting on the end of the counter. "Is that pie over there fresh?"

"Well," the waitress said, planting a hand on her jutting hip, "it may have been when the truck dropped it off two days ago."

Clara just smiled.

"Hey look sweetie, go ahead, huh. I'm just joking; I mean, what's it going to hurt?" She brought over the coffee and set it down in front of Clara. "Life's short, yeah? Live a little; that's what I say." And then she backed off, leaving Clara there with her coffee.

It was good; hot, and strong. She alternated blowing across it and taking sips. The rich smell filled her nose. She sipped it in like some necessary medicine, before setting the cup back down to look around inside. A couple of loners, one masked behind a newspaper, sat in opposite corners. Two teenage girls gleefully caught up in conversation—the only voices to be heard—and their food seemingly untouched in front of them. One of the kitchen staff came out from behind the partition and stood in front of the plate glass windows, rubbing his hands in a towel while he watched the traffic roll by outside.

An old couple was sitting next to one another on one side of a window booth nearest the door. They were both dressed im-peccably for a Friday afternoon—he in a brown wool suit with tie and felt hat, she in a light conservative country-style dress, her shoulders covered in a shawl. Clara watched them, and it became obvious that the couple were not entirely well. He was very slowly placing small forkfuls of food to her mouth, his spotted hand ribbed with thick purple veins, shaking slightly; she was chewing as if it was a reflex, staring off everywhere but here, waxen. After each mouthful, the old man would lower the fork and then wipe her mouth with a napkin. And then they would begin again.

Clara sat silently and watched. How long had they been to-gether? she wondered. She watched the care that the old man was taking with each bite, how he held one hand under her chin as he brought up another mouthful. Was this their big night out? Had it always been their time together, set aside, routine, a tradition of sorts, the rest of their week spent alone in their home? She was transfixed watching them—the beauty of their dance, its naturalness. It was like seeing a painting come alive: still life as real life, a soft, quiet beauty that required attentiveness. She thought of the effort that it must take each day, day after day, to keep going, for one to not let the other fall behind—the love that must exist between them. Clara turned and motioned for the waitress.

"Yes, sweetie?"

"I've changed my mind," Clara said. "I'm going to go ahead and have a piece of that pie."

Jesus H. Christ, Little, what were you thinking?" The chief shifted his heft in the chair, squinting at him through his off-the-rack pharmacy glasses.

"Well, sir, when I arrived on the scene I first made a preliminary assessment of the situation ..."

"Wait, wait, wait, wait. Let me stop you right there." The chief was leaning forward now and pointing a finger at him. "You say you were 'assessing the situation,' huh? Well, I'd like to know," he cleared his throat, " ... what I'd like to know is, and by all accounts so far, this fellow we're looking for, the one who shot you, okay? This fellow was wearing a costume, had tripped in the big shoes and hit his head on the door frame, and was lying on the ground next to the money bag when you arrived on scene. Does that sound right so far?"

Officer Nelson Little nodded.

"Okay, well, from what we're hearing, and you understand there's a whole parking lot full of eyewitnesses, what we're hearing is you turned your back on this fellow. When what you should have been doing, and listen up here, Little, okay, what you should have done was cuff that SOB and make the arrest. But no!" The chief raised his voice now, sat back, and threw his arms up. "No. You're not doing that, are you? What are you doing, huh? *Assessing the situation.* Jesus H. Christ."

They just sat there for a minute: the chief slumped in a visitor chair and Officer Little propped up in the bed.

"If I can add, sir," he scooted forward a bit, sitting up straight, "my primary concern was with the safety and well-being of the citizens on scene."

"Oh, well, of course! The *citizens*! And do you know that while you were, what, checking to see if anyone needed a band aid, the real criminal got away. And you know what the funny thing is, Little?" The chief was pointing again. "Huh? It's going to be those same citizens who expect us to get this guy!" He was drumming his fingers on the arm of the chair.

Officer Little thought for a minute before speaking. "Do we have any leads on this case so far, sir?"

The chief was shaking his head. "We found the real Mouse-Man tied to a chair in his apartment. Told us he woke up that evening to go to work, and someone brained him right off— never really got a look at whoever did it. In the restaurant, well, it was just a big mouse that whipped out a gun, took the money, and ran. That's it so far." The chief looked beat. "Do you have any idea what a mess this is, Little? Do you? Not only do we have a crime that has drawn statewide attention, and no real leads, but the only new business that has come into this town over the last couple of years is now second-guessing their decision to locate here. Hmmgh."

"Well, sir, when they let me out of here, I'm going to make it a top priority to see that the perpetrator is apprehended." Officer Little never looked more serious.

"See that the perpetrator is apprehended? Christ almighty, Little, no one talks like that, okay?" The chief shook his head again. "What you're gonna do, and listen to me here, Little, what you're going to do is get better and get back to work. Every day you're in here playing martyr cop is another day I have to pull someone off needed duty to fill your role on the street. You got that?" He stood up. "And one more thing, Little. Have you been talking to anyone from the newspaper?"

"No, sir."

"Good. Don't. Somehow they heard you were trying to help that girl, when we both know damn well what you should have been doing, and they've interpreted it like you were protecting her from the gunman. You know, hero cop sells papers, I guess, whatever. Either way, it works for us."

"Yes, sir." He was thinking. He needed to get back out there. He was needed. He was looking directly at the chief, eyes narrowed, and head nodding.

"Jesus H. Christ." The chief turned and walked out of the room. There wouldn't be any more visitors.

Officer Little was still sitting up in bed when the nurse came into the room.

"Excuse me, please?" he said. "I've got to get out of here as soon as possible. I'm a policeman, and there's some very important work I need to attend to."

"Yeah, I heard what you two were talking about." She was suppressing a smile in the corners of her mouth. "What you need to do, honey, is sit back and rest; let that hand of yours heal." She pulled the covers up over his legs. "Go on now; just sit back and look out the window."

The hospital was one of the tallest buildings in town, and Officer Nelson Little was up on the top floor looking out over everything. As he watched the sun going down it did look special—his town. He felt his arm prickle.

"Hey," he said, turning in time to see the nurse pulling out the needle.

"Don't you worry, honey," said the nurse, putting her hand on his chest and guiding him back against propped-up pillows. "You just rest here, and I'll be back to check on you in a couple of hours."

Rubbing his arm where he had the shot, he felt his whole body begin to prickle. The lights were coming on all over town now, and he sat there smiling to himself looking out the window at them. He had to remember to ask the doctor about getting out of here as soon as possible. He also had to see about getting a copy of that newspaper.

* * *

By any measure, it was a beautiful town. Nestled in the valley between two mountain ranges, their faraway spines lining two of the four horizons, it was cut off from the encroaching sprawl of development that was spreading across other areas in the state. Of course, while this helped retain small-town charm, it did little to help retain relevance. As far as being a consideration when planning where to start a family, or start a business, or just about anything else, for that matter, if it meant staying in town, it just didn't rank for most folks. It was where you were from, not where you were going.

It wasn't always like that, though.

Near the end of the century, the industrial magnates had seized on its central location between population centers in the northeast corridor. With train lines running straight through the town, and a solid, largely nonitinerant workforce willing to live on a base wage, they came calling with big plans and bigger pocketbooks. There was money to be made. The railroads built a hub and interconnected lines to get from here to everywhere. Steel Inc. saw low overhead and cheap access to the rest of the country as an opportunity too good to pass up. No stone went unturned as mine after mine tore into the landscape. Flush with money in a country hungry for more, to be where the American dream was being manufactured on an industrial scale was to be where the American dream was being realized. It was a self-fulfilling prophecy, and there didn't seem to be any stopping the progress of a nation. Housing, schools, culture, all the signs of economic growth, are the calling card for those who want to raise their stock in life. They are also a bellwether for vitality.

Lesson learned: if the applied science of economics, like the real science of physics, abhors a vacuum, alas the same can be said for the coffers of finance. It was suddenly a new day in America, and their underwear was being sewn together in a grass hut on the Mekong Delta.

The fix was in.

The road into the future became a decline cushioned by the broken dreams of those who continued to believe. The mines pushed farther away and so did the jobs. As the mills went from five foundries to one, labor followed suit. The trains now passed on through, and so did most folks these days.

Despair and anger, tempered by drugs and alcohol, became a constant threat, and in some cases, a way of life. Attempts were made to forestall what seemed at times to be the inevitable, unenviable, conclusion. A community college was built, providing a glimpse of "something else"—a proud investment in the lives of their children, and a secret hope of perhaps nurturing a sentinel, someone who would one day return and save them.

*   *   *

He awoke with a start. The lights were off in the room. The door was shut. Through the window moon-light bathed him in a blue-white glow. Still groggy from whatever the nurse gave him, he smacked his tongue around in his mouth, in need of a drink. His left hand was throbbing.

What time is it? he thought.

He sat up, turned, and hung his legs over the edge of the bed. A carafe of water and a glass were on the nightstand. He poured a tall one, nearly draining it in one long pull. The clock read two in the morning. He sat there for a long minute staring out the window, before standing and moving in closer for a better look.

The town below was lit up like strewn holiday lights, twinkling in the inky darkness. Scattered sets of headlights were making their way through the maze of buildings and trees. In the distance he could make out the red glow from the blast furnace, the late shift pouring long into the night. A train whistle blew low, almost mournfully, cutting through the night air.

Clara stood naked in front of the upstairs bedroom window and let the moon illuminate her. In the dark, she could see well beyond the suburban boundaries of her surroundings, the horizon running up against city lights in the distance, red and white against a black sky. She should have felt safe, secure, at home.

She did not.

He had been too busy to have dinner with her. He had been too busy to ask about her day. He had been too busy to ask her about it. In fact, since their initial conversation, there seemed to have been an unspoken consensus to move on. How did that work? She is going through each day consumed by the knowledge, and the lack of knowledge, the dread, about it. He never mentions it. He has his IT, and she has her "it."

"Same language," she frowned, "different conversation." Choking slightly, she reached for her cigarettes.

Sliding each latch open, she pushed up the sash, leaned down sideways, and swung her leg out the window. Dipping her head under the frame, she came out fully onto the eave over the front entrance, stood up, and walked to the top of the roof.

A warm breeze swirled around her. She closed her eyes and for a moment and swooned, flying away. The grit of the roofing shingles felt good under bare feet, and she ground them around slightly, letting them scrape. She lit a cigarette, balanced the pack and lighter on the peak, and drew in a deep breath. Up here under the sky, she allowed herself to stare at it.

She was confused and afraid.

Afraid that somehow, possibly, she had wasted her life. She was afraid that she was beyond the point of no return: too old to change, undeserving of another chance. Had she squandered her opportunity for something better, something good, something meaningful? Had she opted for a life of convenience and comfort, and missed the point entirely? If there even was a point. Why had she not thought about any of this before? She remembered reading something one time that "nothing focuses the mind like a hanging." Was that it?

Was the clock ticking?

Of course the clock was ticking. It was ticking for everyone whether you paid it any mind or not. Silly girl. It was what you did with your time, or your time left, that counted.

The breeze picked up again. She opened her eyes and watched the cigarette pack tip, slide down the roof and sail over the gutter, silently falling to the yard. It landed with a soft "poof" in the grass.

That ... is not a good sign, she thought.

*   *   *

The flip-flop kept slipping on her foot and was making it hard to level the accelerator, so she kicked them off and drove barefoot. She'd gone back in the house, thrown on some shorts and a T-shirt, grabbed her work smock and the keys, and slipped out the front door. One minute she was retrieving her cigarettes from the yard, and the next she was in the car releasing the brake and rolling it backward down the driveway and into the street.

What if she really was sick? What if she went back to the clinic and signed on for the whole program: the diagnosis, the surgery, the treatment. What if she fought and lost?

"Am I ready for that? Is *this* enough?"

She slowed the car down when she realized she didn't have her license or any ID with her. She glanced at the clock: two in the morning. An all-night convenience store was up ahead, and she pulled into the parking lot. Digging around in the armrest compartment, she came up with enough change to buy a coffee.

A very tall man was behind the counter with a very long beard, wearing a very large turban, who followed her in and around the store with a penetrating and expressionless eye. The entire store was filled with the aroma of brewed coffee, and she probably could have found it with her eyes closed. With the decanter still gurgling, she poured a cup, popped on a lid and brought her change to the counter. Staring at his name tag first, "Hi, I'm Shikra," she then met his gaze and handed over the money. He reached out, dropped his eyes to her breast plate, and read the embroidered "Clara" on her smock, before ringing up the sale.

Clara and Shikra then took a moment to just be in each other's silent presence, before he finally bowed his head slightly, she smiled slightly, and they parted ways forever.

* * *

Back on the road, Clara was driving. Not to anywhere, but just driving.

Driving herself freaking crazy, she thought. "Fuck!" she yelled out through the window as she roared down the highway. "If you're not going to do the smart thing," her anger flaring, "then what the hell are you going to do?"

Coming over a rise, she could see something in the road. Slowing down, she pulled up and stopped behind a car that had pulled over to the curb. She turned off the engine, got out, and saw that there were at least three other vehicles all stopped in the roadway up ahead. A man was lying in the street. A car was sitting at a wrong angle on the other side of the intersection. A couple of people were standing alongside each spot. Clara pocketed the keys and made her way over.

A lanky Rastafarian, a green and yellow blanket thrown around his shoulders, was on his back in the crosswalk. His eyes were open, and his dreadlocks splayed out around his head like some giant tarantula with a face tattooed on its back.

He was smiling.

"He was walking with the signal when that man over there," a lady standing there told Clara as she approached, "well, he went right through the red light, hit this man here, and then crashed into the phone pole over there." She was pointing across the intersection. "I was right here and saw the whole thing." She leaned in closer to Clara. "They say it looks like he's been drinking." She frowned through her heavy glasses and shook her head.

Clara looked across the road where two men were attempting to help what did indeed appear to be an inebriated third man, get out of his damaged vehicle. The third man was making a loud kind of slurring ruckus as they walked him over to the sidewalk.

"Has anyone called for an ambulance?" asked Clara.

"I did," said a man leaning on a car still stopped at the intersection proper. "They should be here soon."

Leaning down toward the man in the road, Clara asked, "Are you all right? Does it hurt anywhere?"

"I … will be fine," said the man, an air of pride in his voice.

Clara got down on her hands and knees next to him. The others gathered around to watch. "Is there anything we can do for you?"

The man grinned even wider. "You smell like smoke. I would like a cigarette, if you have an extra one?" He looked at her embroidered smock. "Clara."

"You know," said the spectacled lady, "I'm not sure that's a good idea."

Clara looked at her and then back at him.

"Today is not a good day, so far," the Rasta said. "It may get better, though. There is still time." He smiled again.

Clara took out her pack, lit a cigarette, and placed it in the man's mouth. Something about the way he smoked made

Clara think it was a reflection of how he lived his life: a long powerful draw that seemed to half the length in only one inhalation. A seed popped and showered bits of tobacco and spark onto his neck. Excess smoke that leaked through his partially open lips was caught and drawn back in through his nostrils. He closed his eyes and exhaled.

"Thank you, Clara," he said. "My name is Marcus."

"Marcus, is there anyone we could call for you, to let them know what's happened?"

"Thank you, Clara, but no. I am a lone voyager in this life. I will be fine."

The ambulance arrived, and Clara stood back along with everyone else and let them attend to Marcus. *It may get better,* she replayed his words in her mind. *There is still time.* As she watched Marcus being loaded onto the stretcher, she couldn't help thinking for a minute that he'd been talking to her, that she was supposed to hear that. As the paramedic wheeled him over to the ambulance, Clara approached.

"Marcus, will you be all right? Do you have money, any insurance?" she asked.

He was smiling.

As they prepared to close the ambulance doors behind him, Marcus looked over at her. "Don't be a silly girl, Clara. There are no gua-ran-tees in this life."

She realized that she had come to a decision the minute she stopped thinking about it. Clara pulled into the drive-way knowing that one way or another, this would be it. She left the engine running and climbed out.

Someone's going to ask me where I've been.

She looked up at the sky—the sun would be coming up in an hour or so. She walked onto the front porch, put her key in the lock, and entered the house, leaving the door wide open.

Someone's going to ask me what's going on.

The house was dark. From across the room she could make out the blue light pouring out from under a door down the hallway. She listened but could hear nothing. The house was silent. She made no effort to cover her being there and strode into the kitchen, pulled open the refrigerator door, and, after pushing some bottles around, pulled out a soda-pop.

Someone's going to ask me if I'm all right.

In front of the sink, she snapped off the cap and took a sip. Outside the window she could see the moon disappearing behind the trees. She reached over and squirted some dishwashing detergent into the palm of her hand. Running the tap, she then vigorously scrubbed her hands and face, splashing water to rinse. With eyes closed, she tipped her head back, splayed her fingers, and combed the hair back over her head, exhaling slowly.

Someone's going to ask me how I'm feeling.

She tore off a paper towel and ran it across her face and the back of her neck. Then, balling it up, she pitched it toward the trash can, where it bounced off the rim and fell onto the floor. She stared at it for a moment before turning and walking out.

Someone's going to ask if there is anything they can do for me.

She stood and looked again down the hall, at the door closed to her. She trudged up the stairs, went into the bedroom, opened the closet, pushed aside the hanging clothing, reached to the back wall, and pulled out her old tote bag. Tossing it onto the edge of the bed, she unzipped the main compartment and looked inside: a small first aid kit, her camera, a tiny flashlight, some empty plastic bags, and a handful of receipts from … what? The last time she'd been on a vacation? When was that, five years ago? She poured everything out onto the bed, tossed the first aid kit back in, grabbed one of the plastic bags, and went into the bathroom.

Someone will ask me what am I doing and where am I going.

Opening the medicine cabinet, she scanned the contents before reaching over and scooping the entire lower shelf into the bag. She walked back into the bedroom and dropped the bag into her tote. She noticed that the window was still open and walked over, sticking her head out. The car was still in the driveway, engine running, lights on, and door open. The sky was transforming, its deepness thinning. She turned back in.

Someone will ask me if I'm crazy. What am I thinking?

A handful of underwear, a couple of tops, a couple of pants, some socks, and a pair of hard shoes; roll them up and squish them all in. She stood thinking before going back to the closet. Leafing through some hangers, she pulled off a sleeveless sundress, which she carefully rolled up, put into one of the plastic bags and placed on top of the tote's contents.

Someone will ask me how I can do this. Why would I do this?

Satisfied, she zipped the tote shut, slung it over her shoulder, grabbed her purse off the dresser, and left the room. She stopped in the front doorway and turned back, looking into the house.

Someone will stop me, throw their arms around me, and hold me.

She walked to the car. Getting in, she tossed the tote over the back of the seat and dropped her purse onto the floor next to her. She slammed the door shut and revved the engine once. Putting it in gear, she backed out of the driveway and into the street, where she then shifted the transmission into park and just sat there with the engine running.

She rolled down the window and dug her cigarettes out of her smock's pocket. Directly ahead through the windshield the sun was about to rise. She smoked and stared directly at it.

Someone will tell me that they love me.

The first beam of light, for just a moment, shot straight up, and then tipped forward like a falling tree. She was beginning to squint now as the shower of light rose over the horizon. *It's breathing*, she thought.

Looking back at the house through the passenger-side window, she saw a huge bird, one that she had never seen before, looking at her from a tree in the front yard.

Well, that's that.

"Bye-bye," and she put the car into motion.

A spike of anxiety set her teeth chattering, and she bit down. Out of the corner of her eye she looked at the rearview mirror, reached over, and turned it up.

Too late, she said to herself, accelerating.

Do you know what they put in hot dogs," said the old Indian, poking at the grill with a stick. Clara, holding her hot dog with both hands, her mouth full, shook her head. "Sodium nitrate." He stopped and turned to her, "They use that to make fireworks too. Also say it causes cancer."

Clara stopped chewing.

"I like hot dogs," the Indian said. "They taste good, and when you eat one, it reminds you that life also has to be about doing what you like." He went back to poking at the grill. "About going your own way."

She'd been driving all morning, and not having any sleep the night before, had pulled into the rest area to get out and stretch, walk around a bit. The parking lot stayed full as a steady line of cars came and went. The big trucks, on the road all night, lined up out back, engines running and drivers asleep. The old Indian had set up shop on the edge of a picnic area, his beaded jewelry laid out on a folding card table, a paper sack with the wiener packages and a bun bag at his feet. Farther back, under the shade of a tree, an old woman wrapped in a blanket sat on an overturned bucket watching out for him. Clara resumed chewing and slowly browsed the table. A sputtering roar drew her attention back to the parking lot, where a motorcycle rolled in before backfiring once and conking out. Clara stood in the shade eating as she watched the riders dismount and bend over the bike: a big fuzzy bear of a man and his sun-weathered female passenger. They looked none too happy about the now-quiet motorcycle.

Finished with her hot dog, she made her way into the restroom to clean up. It wasn't much past noon, and yet by the look of it, half the state had already stopped in to pee on the floor. First making herself a seat cover with toilet paper, and then flushing with her foot, she washed up, and had no choice but to punch the blow dryer, and immediately felt she needed to wash again.

I can't be the only one who hates these things, she thought.

And she did, only this time reentering the stall and pulling off a big handful of tissue paper, drying, and then using it to open the door, tossing it back toward the trash can on her way out. It missed, and she left it.

On her way back to her car, she paused again at the old Indian's table, where the motorcycle passenger was looking over a piece of his work. She was holding what looked like a broach, a black horse running against a red background. She noted Clara's presence by turning it to show her.

"I could use some of this mojo right about now," she said, smiling. Turning back to the Indian, "I'll take it. How much?"

While the biker lady and the Indian haggled, Clara browsed again, not realizing she'd been daydreaming until a hand entered her line of sight and slowly pointed to a hair barrette—a brown hawk floating across a white background. Her eyes turned up and into the face of the Indian. He was inexpressive lifting the barrette off the table with one hand and taking her hand with the other. Pressing the jewelry into her palm, he folded her fingers over and across it.

"You be careful out there on the road," he told her.

She stood there with her hand in his, firm and coarse. He shook their hands just slightly before releasing his grip and turning back to the grill. She looked over to the old lady under the trees, who was now sitting erect, staring directly at her. Clara mouthed *thank you* before heading off back to her car.

Once again behind the wheel, Clara pulled her hair back, secured it in place with the barrette, and rolled down all the windows. *Another couple of hours of this*, she thought, and pulled back out onto the interstate.

* * *

She had driven for several more hours until she just couldn't pass up another motel. Calling it a day, she'd gotten a room, freshened up, and then crossed the street to get something to eat.

It was one of those twenty-four-hour restaurants catering to the needs of travelers: an odds and ends shop stocking everything from no-doze pills and hemorrhoid relief creams to duct tape and mosquito repellant, plenty of lockers and showers and a diner full of Formica tabletops with red pleather booths. Clara had only just taken a seat before her two new admirers began staring, trying to draw her attention from their perch at the bar.

She picked up a menu, turning her back to them, and pretended to look it over, keeping watch by the reflection in the glass windows. *They're readying themselves*, she thought, seeing them pointing their chins in her direction. She began to feel a little queasy as they left the bar, headed her way.

They walked over single file, each holding a beer, each dressed in what appeared to be the same business suit. They stopped side by side across the front of her booth, blocking her in. They were oblivious to their obviousness and *obviously drunk*, was her first thought when she finally looked up at them.

"Excuse us," said the businessman through red flickering eyes, "but we couldn't help noticing you over here. We're uhh …," he almost smirked, "we're just traveling through here tonight on business."

Eyeing them skeptically, Clara felt the disgust register across her face before she dropped her head, still holding the menu with both hands. *Please go away*, she thought.

"Hey, look," said the businessman, "you don't have to act like that." He slid into the booth next to her. "We're just looking for a good time, you know, looking for some," he glanced up at his partner, "some company, you know." He reached out and put his hand on Clara's shoulder.

"Don't touch me!" she shouted, smacking him in the face with the laminated menu and recoiling farther around the booth. Her shoulders rose around her neck, and she closed her eyes, turning away.

The businessman slid out and rose onto his feet, sneering through smiling teeth at her. "You small-town types are all alike." The two of them stood there in front of her bobbing slightly, their shoulders bumping. "Money, I suppose, huh? You want to know how much we ..."

And the talking stopped.

Clara sat there breathing heavily through her nose, eyes closed, head down. After a moment, when it seemed safe, she looked up. The businessmen were still there, only they were now looking past her. She turned and saw that a man had positioned himself next to her booth. The businessmen were staring at him, not saying anything. He seemed somehow familiar, and Clara stared too.

It was the bear on the motorcycle from the rest stop. His beard obscured the entire lower half of his face; the upper was situated behind thick-lensed glasses, giving him the appearance of a pony-tailed owl. He stood there as still as if a great tree had suddenly taken root right there in the middle of the diner. No one spoke; no one moved. Clara looked around the room and saw the motorcycle lady waving her over to their booth.

She never looked back, except to notice the reflection in the glass window of the biker moving in to say something to the businessmen. Somehow, she thought she wouldn't be seeing them again.

"Are you okay, honey?" said the motorcycle lady. "You'll sit here with us, okay?" She scooted over to make room.

So Clara, Gina, and Big Ed had dinner together: BLTs with thick slabs of bacon and lots of yellow mustard, onion rings, sour dill pickles, and a pitcher of sweet tea. They talked a lot, laughed a lot, and ate a lot. Clara hadn't eaten anything except that Indian's hot dog since she'd left home, and she sat back and luxuriated in the cozy atmosphere. An overhead fan was moving the air, cool and slow; the sound of dishes and glasses clinking from the kitchen mixed with the jukebox radio, songs she'd never heard before mixed with the occasional soundtrack from her youth. Several times she'd caught herself swaying along to the music. When their table was cleared, both she and Gina had a piece of key lime pie and a cup of coffee; Big Ed finished off the rest and then put his head back and dozed in place. Clara and Gina went out front and lit up their cigarettes.

"So we're going home," said Gina, "after all these years."

She put her head back and blew a line of smoke straight up. "You know, at first we didn't know what to do, after Eddie got let go. But then we thought about it, and you know what?" She looked at Clara. "For all the time that we'd been in that city, I couldn't remember even once where it ever felt real, like it fit, like it was home. Do you know what I mean?"

Clara nodded. *Oh yeah, kind of,* she thought to herself.

"Eddie worked for that company, doing all their engine work, weekends, holidays, nights, you name it, keeping their damn delivery trucks on the road for the better part of thirty years. And you know what it got him in the end?"

Clara shook her head.

"A retirement plan that had been frozen in place ten years ago and a 401k plan that's worth less than half what it was ten years ago." She looked frustrated, angry. She looked like she might cry.

"You know, those bastards told him to clear out his stuff right then and there, letting everyone go, subleasing the delivery end to a contractor for half the expense. It's terrible."

She was looking at Big Ed through the glass.

"Some of those guys have families, small kids. I mean Ed and me, well, we'll get by, be okay, but what in the hell are some of the rest of them going to do? Those bastards oughtta be ashamed of themselves." She flicked her cigarette butt into the parking lot and promptly lit another.

Clara followed suit, lighting a new one off of what was left from the other. "Gina, do you mind if I ask how long you and Ed have been together?"

"Oh, well, you know God bless his soul," Gina said, her eyes tearing up. "Eddie and I grew up together. Since we were just little kids, up north in the timberlands just this side of the border."

She had put her hand on the glass door, palm flat, and was looking directly across the restaurant at him. Big Ed, for his part, was still napping, head back and arms straight out in front of him on the table. Clara saw two small boys laughing and pointing at him from an adjacent booth. One of them threw a french fry, and it landed on Big Ed's forehead. It just sat there rising and falling with his breathing. Gina laughed quietly.

"You know, he saved my life," Gina said, turning back to face Clara. "You might not be able to tell now, but when I was younger," and she laughed again, "I was a real looker. A real party girl. Truth was, a real mess, if I'm being honest." She shook her head.

"You name it—drugs, drinking, all manner of carrying on—I didn't miss much. Hell, I cheated on Eddie with too many to remember, and cheated on just as many with him. Like I said, a real mess."

She finished the cigarette and watched its red trail as it sailed out onto the blacktop. "And then one day, thirty years ago, you know, he put me on the back of that same damn motorcycle and drove me down here with him, looking for work. He gave me a chance to get clean, start over."

She stared off across the parking lot.

"So, yeah, now we're going home. Only now it won't matter what happens, you know? I'm with that big oaf until the end, no matter what, and I can't imagine being any happier."

*　*　*

Later that night, lying on the bed in her motel room, Clara thought back to what Gina had said about being with Big Ed, until the end, *no matter what*. She thought about her marriage and wondered if she was making a mistake. She took the remote control and turned on the television—a news report about a cop shot, while protecting a child at a birthday party, by a costumed gunman on the loose and considered dangerous. She turned the television off.

How absurd, she thought to herself. *What on earth is the world coming to?*

*　*　*

The next morning, just before dawn, Clara awoke to the sound of a motorcycle firing up, it's idle popping and crackling in the motel parking lot. Finally she heard it moving and then a long winding roar as it sped off into the morning. She lay there listening until she couldn't make it out any more.

How absurd, she thought. *What on earth is my life coming to?*

It was time to get up. She hoped to be at her sister's house before evening.

She hoped to be home.

The rookie sat behind the wheel of the police cruiser and stared at Officer Nelson Little with a look of disbelief. "For god's sake, Little, will you get your head back in the window? You look like some dog going down the highway." He shook his head. "Do you know how stupid that makes us look?"

Since being released from the hospital, and because his left hand was still stitched together and wrapped in gauze, Officer Little had been reassigned to ride along with the rookie—"mentoring" they called it down at the station. Initially he had been assigned a desk at the station, but after a couple of days of that ended with the chief needing to be checked for a possible aneurism, whispered to be the result of Officer Little's constant suggestions on procedural improvements, a large purple blotch had formed next to the chief's eye, and it was determined to get Officer Little back out in the field by any means necessary.

"Hey, what's wrong with you anyway, Little?" The rookie scrunched up his face for further emphasis.

"I would say that I'm more than fine and that there isn't anything wrong with me, rook."

"Geez, and why don't you stop callin' me 'rook', huh?" said the rookie.

"Sure thing ... rook." Officer Little nodded his head and ha-ha'd to no one in particular.

"God, Little, you're an idiot."

*   *   *

They'd been together now for two days, nearly twenty hours, and it had been a fairly slow week by police standards. Still, Officer Little had taken every opportunity to show the rookie real on-the-ground police work wherever he deemed it appropriate. It had, for the most part, gone well, he thought. There was the anomaly of clearing out those Girl Scouts who'd been selling cookies under the No Loitering sign in front of the grocery store, whereby someone had then thrown a Samoa at him, and the rookie had let him walk around the rest of the morning with it stuck to the back of his shirt. But he was even able to use that as an example of better policing: teamwork means watching each other's back. Later at lunch Officer Little had not let on that he had seen the rookie take a pickle slice off his hamburger and throw it at his back. He'd simply excused himself under the guise of a bathroom break, cleaned off the condiment, and returned ready to go. He figured it was a learning curve and that the rookie was a good kid; he'd figure it out.

"Hey, you know, Little, you know what I'm thinkin'?" The rookie was speeding around the other cars on the road now, using the police car to his advantage, intimidating. "I'm thinking that maybe this assignment with you might turn out to be the best thing that could have happened for me, you know that?"

"Well, I'm glad that's how you feel, rook. Thanks for that."

"No, I'm serious Little. I mean I'd heard about this lawman-persona around the station, you know." He turned and looked at Officer Little, making a mock face of extreme seriousness. "Letter of the law and all that. But to see it in person, geez no one would believe it if I told 'em." He turned back and looked at the road ahead. "You're a real piece of work, Little, a complete regulations asshole. No wonder everyone hates you back at the station." He turned again and smiled at Officer Little.

"Rookie, I think you're mistaken. Those men and I have been around the block a few times together, seen a lot of things, not all of them good. It's a bond, a brotherhood, if you will." He was looking off out the window.

"Yeah, right," said the rookie.

"Look, rook, you might learn something here." He was being serious. "In this line of work sometimes the only release can be achieved in the company of those who'd understand, who'd know." He was steely; his voice had dropped a register. "You can't take it home; you can't talk it out with your friends. They just wouldn't get it. So," and he reached over and slapped the rookie's shoulder, "you josh around with the team—diffuse your emotions, decompress. You get it?"

"Oh yeah, I get it, all right. You're not just an idiot; you're a clueless idiot." He was back to scrunching up his face. "Hey, Little, do me a favor, huh? Don't touch me again. Okay?"

"Take it easy, rook. I know, it's a bitter pill, the truth." He was pointing his bandaged hand at the rookie now. "You'll come around. Your eyes will clear, and you'll see it for what it is."

"See it for what it is? Oh, man, you really are delusional." He was shaking his head again. "Look, Little, when we came through the station this morning and everyone was raising their left hands up with fingers parted and telling you to 'live long and prosper,' what do you think they were doing, huh?"

Officer Little put out both hands in front of him. "Solidarity among the team."

"Solidarity! Holy shit, Little, who do you think you are, huh? Lech Walesa? They're fucking with you, man. You're Spock, an alien." He was laughing now.

"Hey, rook," Officer Little said. "You ever heard the phrase 'can't see the forest for the trees'?"

The rookie stared at him. "God, Little, you're an idiot."

*   *   *

They'd been given the task of delivering failure to appear summonses. Considered routine police work, that was an oxymoron if there ever was one. Routine police work, like Internet security, was an oft-used phrase with no basis in reality. It was all free doughnuts and coffee at the Quick-Mart, until the shooting starts. The two policemen had spent their morning delivering one summons after another for a variety of offenses deemed unworthy of revisitation by the accused. Needless to say, it was a long morning.

"Okay, rook, where to next?" said Officer Little as he leafed through the logbook.

"Manny Hernandez, for unauthorized use of handicap parking."

"Really?" Officer Little looked up, "You mean Manny Hernandez the drug dealer?"

"No, Little," said the rookie. "I mean Manny Hernandez, suspected drug dealer, convicted parking offender." He looked over at Officer Little. "Dial it back, Little, okay? This guy's not to be messed with, and we don't need any of your moralizing getting us marked. You know? Geez."

But Officer Little wasn't listening to the rookie. He was pouring over the initial charge sheet. Hernandez was known throughout the town as its only distributor of illegal narcotics. He'd been investigated so many times, and nothing ever stuck for a conviction. *This is it*, thought Officer Little. He was going right to the man's residence with the full power of the law behind him—parking in a designated handicap space could be the falling domino that brings the whole operation down. He'd read of things like this before and sensed this was his time. He had the thousand-yard stare going.

"Hey, snap out of it, Little," said the rookie. "You're starting to freak me out, okay? What are you thinking over there, huh? Don't be stupid, let's just deliver the summons and go about our way. Let the courts handle it from there."

The two policemen pulled up in front of a slightly ramshackle house surrounded by a chain-link fence. The rookie pulled the cruiser over to the curb in front and shut off the engine. They looked at one another across the front seat of the vehicle.

"Man you're too much," said the rookie. "Give me that log-book," and he reached over and snatched it out of Officer Little's hands. "What are you planning on doing, marching up there on false pretenses and busting this guy's whole network? You're crazy." He turned his back on Officer Little and opened the car door. "You wait here, and I'll go up and deliver the summons."

"Sure thing, rook," said Officer Little, as he opened his door and stepped out.

Officer Little took the lead, grabbing back the logbook as he came around the rookie from behind. With his head held high, and after hitching up his pants with one hand, he opened the gate and stepped into the yard.

Things went sideways almost immediately.

He didn't see the first dog until it was nearly on him. It hadn't made a sound, no yelping or barking, complete silence, running fast and low to the ground. It hit him with the force of a sandbag being dropped on top of him. Officer Little rolled as he'd been taught in his own rookie training days and took a knee. They were everywhere, streaming out from behind the house. He saw the rookie scramble back, falling over the fence onto the safety of the sidewalk. He turned back around in time to see the next dog move in and clamp it's snout down into the bandages on his hand.

"*Noooo!*" he shouted as he stumbled backward into the teaming pile. The dog in question, with its hindquarters still standing, almost bowed down with its front legs as it twisted its head and made eye contact through the bouquet of bandages it had in its mouth.

The front door to the house opened, and a man with a shotgun stepped out onto the front porch.

Instinct at that point prompted Officer Nelson Little to reach for his own sidearm. It was another dog behind him, which he didn't see, that tripped him up, causing him to fall over backward, and it was the impact of his head making contact with the concrete walkway that caused him to, for the first time in a professional capacity, discharge his service weapon. He was pointing his gun straight up into the air, lying on his back, when just before blacking out he saw the rookie on the other side of the fence shaking his head, silently mouthing words he couldn't quite make out.

* * *

When he came to, a paramedic was kneeling over him. "Welcome back," he said while rebandaging Little's hand. "You're a lucky guy. When we first got here you looked a mess, you know, your hand and all. But," and he turned to look Officer Little in the face, "you're not too bad, at least comparatively speaking. According to your boss there," and he pointed to the front porch, "you've had quite the week."

Officer Little looked in the direction of the house and saw the chief among a group of officers and civilians on the front porch, looking at him from a distance, hands in his pockets, chewing something.

"Yeah, I'd say you're going to be okay. You got bit twice, both times on your leg here," and the paramedic showed him where they'd cut off his left pant leg to dress the bites, "but they're superficial at best—should heal nice and quick. Given your recent hospital stay, you won't even need another tetanus shot. Speaking of which," and he held up Officer Little's freshly wrapped left hand, "you really ought to try and take better care of this, at least what's left of it."

With that the paramedic turned away to reveal the chief standing there, involuntarily rubbing the purple splotch on his temple, frowning at him. Officer Little made to speak when the chief cut him off.

"Not now, Little," he said, holding up his hand. "The accidental discharge of a firearm while in the process of serving a summons related to a class one misdemeanor punishable by up to a twenty dollar fine? Really, Little? Jesus H. Christ." He turned sideways, looking out toward the road, and put his hands back in his pockets. "I called your mother, dear poor Edna. What she ever did to deserve all this I'll never understand, but I told her what happened. She's expecting you. Clean up, Little, take a couple of days off, and get it together. We'll get you a ride. Go home." Without looking back, he walked off toward the jam of cruisers in the street.

Officer Nelson Little sat there in the grass—bandaged hand, gauze taped to his leg, the smell of gun powder still in his nose from the discharge, pants torn. That was a full day, he thought.

"I'm coming home."

Clara knew where she was going, could feel where she was going, but couldn't bring it to the front of her consciousness. She couldn't allow that. If she did, then she'd make an excuse, she knew it. She'd go back to her parent's house, back to Mara's house, and sit there watching television until sleep overtook her.

So she kept walking.

Streets she'd been up and down hundreds of times, in what seemed like a hundred years ago, hadn't changed a bit. Weathered but holding their own, tiny houses huddled together block after block as if gathering to ward off an unseen onslaught. The sodium filaments hummed in the street fixtures above as she made her way from one pool of vapor to the next.

She was awash in illumination without any clarification.

So she kept going, kept walking.

At the railroad crossing she stopped and listened. At first it was a sound that she couldn't hear. Slowly her feet buzzed in her shoes, and finally the small hairs on her arms rose up. She looked both ways, unable to tell, and when the first red lamp snapped on, bathing her in its iridescence, it was as if there was a drop in the air pressure, the barometer in her mind actuating events in front of her eyes. It felt huge. When the bells started ringing, and the gates dropped, a shudder coursed through her body, and she stepped back.

"Here it comes," she told herself.

*   *   *

She'd arrived at her sister's house later than she'd expected. Unannounced, she knocked on the front door, expecting Mara to be surprised. Instead, after pushing open the screen door and looking her over once, she had stood aside and motioned for her to come in.

"I was wondering how long it'd be before you showed up."

Clara's face must have registered puzzlement because before she could explain anything, Mara did.

"Your husband's been calling," she said, "about four times a day by my count." Turning to meet Clara's eyes, she added, "That is unless he's also been at it when I've been at work."

It had been almost two days since she'd left, thought Clara. That was odd, though, the way she hadn't even really thought about him, the way she'd just assumed he'd still be in the home office, unaware and uninterrupted.

"He's probably wondering where his dinner is," Clara said, stepping past her sister and into the house.

"Hey," said Mara, placing her hand flat on the back of Clara's shoulder, "You're okay, huh? I mean, nothing's *really* wrong, is there?"

Clara turned and faced her sister, attempting to mask her thoughts. "It's fine. I'm fine," she said, managing a smile that was undone by the droop in her eyes.

Mara didn't even try to hide her skepticism but pursed her lips and nodded slowly. "Okay. Either way ...," and she kissed her own fingertips and placed them on Clara's forehead like she used to do when they were children, "it's good to see you, sis." And then she waved a hand toward the upstairs bedrooms before turning and making her way back to the kitchen.

*   *   *

Hesitating slightly at first, Clara walked into her room, her own room, the only one, and it felt like a puzzle-piece dropping into place. It may have been devoid of her belongings, but she knew the geometry of it. She could have closed her eyes and described it with a thoroughness unlike anything else in her life: the snowfalls she'd watched through the window, the books she'd read in the sunlight; her sister's radio bleeding through the woodwork, and covers over her head, in bed, listening.

It certainly looked like home.

*   *   *

Next to an old dust-covered bowl of plastic fruit, without a real piece anywhere in sight, Clara sat at the kitchen table frowning while she watched Mara scrape out the last of the spiced ham from a tin and wipe it onto saltine crackers.

"Thank you, Mara."

"Hmm?" Mara, with her mouth full, looked away and shook her hand at Clara before swallowing. "You don't have to, Clara, okay? We'll talk about it tomorrow. Just relax, all right? I have to work in the morning, but if I can I'll leave early, and we'll have the rest of the day together. Sound good?" she said, accenting her point by dinging the rim of a glass soda-pop bottle with her spoon.

*   *   *

The locomotive leaned into the curve and groaned as it approached, its progress measured by the burgeoning headlamps. Clara drew in her breath and, when it was finally on her, stepped forward as close as she dared, threw her head back, and allowed herself to be consumed by its speeding immensity. The silhouette of a man, aglow in green light and leaning out the engine's window high above, acknowledged her presence as he flew past, tipping his hand in her direction. Her vision blurred trying to focus on the motion.

If someone had something they wanted to get rid of, she thought, *they could stand here and throw it up onto the train.*

She closed her eyes.

If someone had something they wanted to get rid of, she wished, *and never see again, then they could stand here and throw it up onto the train.*

And then it was gone, passing her by. She watched as it disappeared, clattering off into the past. She turned back and looked across the tracks at the town beyond.

"If someone had something they wanted to get rid of," she said aloud, "they could stand here and think maybe this was the place."

*   *   *

It was dark, but Clara knew where she was going, physically certain even if she didn't want to think of it directly. She walked between the trees and found that she was reaching out to each one as she passed, letting her hand run along its trunk. As her eyes adjusted, she made sure to be careful where she walked, following the grid, the grass tipped in blue from the moon overhead. Fireflies blinking in the air, the dull chugging of locusts, and a perpetually rising and falling chorus of crickets masked any sense of the town outside the gates.

She stepped up to her father's grave.

"Daddy,'" she said out loud, her voice breaking.

"Daddy, something's wrong. I think something's wrong," and her eyes filled with tears. With her hands clenched, she shook her fists up and down in front of herself.

"I think I'm sick, Daddy," she sobbed, trembling, "I think something's wrong."

She sat down in the grass, leaning forward with her hands outstretched flat before her. Dew soaked through her pants and onto her legs; tears dropped onto her arms.

"Oh my god, I'm scared, Daddy."

She let go, crying.

"I'm afraid something's wrong."

She lay down in the wet grass.

It wasn't the sound of the train that woke him up. He was already awake, or at the very least, not necessarily asleep. Rather it was as good an excuse as any to get up. His leg was sore from the bites, and his hand, gauzed up and wrapped in an old plastic bread bag to keep it from getting pulled apart while tossing around in bed, was throbbing. He sat up slowly, turned, and stood. Immediately the fresh wounds on his leg flared, causing him to bend and limp slightly as he walked over to the window.

*   *   *

On arriving home, his mother had sat parked in her wheelchair at the door, watching him through the screen as he'd made his way up the walk. Shaking her head in a way that he knew only too well, she grabbed her wheels and spun around just as he pulled open the latch. There was minimal conversation that evening as they sat in the tiny kitchen and had dinner together. Afterward he pushed her out into the front room to watch television while he washed dishes and put everything away.

"Mom, would you like it if I made some tea?" he called from the kitchen.

Edna Little turned away from the game show to look at the empty kitchen entranceway.

"No, thank you, Nelson. I wouldn't want to chance your igniting something flammable with the stove on and burning the house down around us. I'll just sit here and watch TV, thanks."

Nelson Little limped into the entranceway with a wet plate in his one good hand and a dish towel thrown over his shoulder.

"Well, I'm glad to see that you've shaken that funk you were in and are back with us here in the land of the living," he said, a wide smile across his face.

"You just be careful out there," Edna said. "You're one accident away from the two of us having to switch places." She turned back to her show. "Lot of good we'll be if we're both rolling around this house."

"Ha-ha-ha" Nelson said to the back of his mother's head. "You make it seem like we're just scraping by, minutes from catastrophe. Ha, you know that nothing could be further from the truth. Besides, a couple of scratches heal, and I'll be back in action by this time next week. Could have happened to anyone," and he went back into the kitchen.

"If you mean," Edna called after him, "that getting your finger shot off at point blank range by a mascot, and then being attacked by an entire pack of hunting dogs all in the same week, could be construed as just another day at the office, then, yes, you're right. Lord have mercy," she said, shaking her head, "I hope no one had their cell phone video on when you were out there making the world safe for us mortals."

Nelson came back to the entranceway. "Okay, now you're just being difficult for difficulty's sake," he responded back. "Are you sure you don't want any tea?"

Edna kept looking at the television, answering, "If you insist."

* * *

Pulling the curtains aside, he could make out the train working its way through the crossing on the end of the block. Leaning on the sill, he let the soothing vibration work its way up his right arm. The flashing warning lights gave the scene a red-hued strobe effect as boxcar after boxcar swam past. He watched dreamily through sleep-encrusted eyes until the caboose passed. As the bell stopped and the lights clicked off, just as he was pulling back from the window, something caught his eye. He stood there in the dark and again leaned, squinting into the glass.

Someone was there.

He couldn't be sure; he couldn't tell. He rubbed his eyes and stared hard. Yes. Yes, someone is there, he thought. They were moving now, walking through the crossing and down the street. Watching, it appeared to be a woman? "Hmmm," he murmured to himself, stepping back from the window.

Wincing as he put weight on his left leg, he made his way to the bathroom. With his head under the faucet he swished around two mouthfuls of water and spit them out before swallowing a third. Then turning the water off and drying his face on a towel, he headed back to his bedroom, slipped under the covers, and shut his eyes.

He sat up and looked at the clock.

2:00 a.m.

At this time of night? What on earth was anyone doing, especially a lone woman, standing in the street at two in the morning watching a train pass? He got back out of bed and went to the window.

No one—they were gone.

Still, *that was unusual*, he was thinking as he rubbed his chin and considered the situation. He stood there in the dark proposing possibilities.

"What if something is wrong, and she needs help?" he said aloud.

That was all it took before Officer Nelson Little, still in his pajamas, put on his shoes, grabbed his keys, and threw on his police jacket. Silently making his way down the hall, he opened the front door and stepped out onto the porch. He again looked down the street and could see no one. Whoever it was had a head start, but, even with his injured leg, he was sure he could catch up, and off he hobbled out to the street.

He'd made his way through the crossing and another three blocks down the road before he came to a stop. He'd seen no one. In the street out in front of the rear entrance to the cemetery he stood, listened, and looked around.

Could they have gone in there? he wondered, looking up the grassy slope toward the tree line. Three other directions and there was nothing except quiet darkness. He turned back toward the cemetery. Why would anyone go in there at this time of night?

Still, he thought, *it can't hurt to check it out*. He made his way over to the edge of the grass and took one more look around before stepping onto the incline.

He was keeping his head straight and eyes focused on the darkening ascent when his right shoe cut a swath through a slick, raised earthen mass, his leg sliding out from under him. He leaned onto his left leg to compensate and felt the eruption of pain flare upward. He lost his balance. Falling over while attempting to keep his left hand elevated, he took the full brunt of the mushy impact on his right side unchecked, sliding back down to the edge of the road.

"Oooooohhhfffff," he audibly blew as all air was expelled from his lungs.

He lay there for a while, the wet, dewy grass soaking his pajamas, as he slowly regained his breath. Finally he sat up, put his hand flat on the ground, lifted himself up a bit, and took a knee.

"Ouch."

Getting to his feet, sore, wet, and breathing through his nose, he again looked up at the grassy slope. After a moment, thinking that it wasn't very likely anyway, he began to make his way back home.

*   *   *

"It had been worth a try," he told himself, as he climbed onto the porch and opened the door. Tracking dog poop across the living room carpet, he made his way back to the bedroom and called it a night.

He fell asleep almost immediately.

Even in the dark, Clara could see that she lay there with both eyes wide open. Staring at the ceiling, appearing not to see anything, or maybe just not looking at anything? Either way there was something about her that Clara couldn't get over, couldn't stop thinking about as she had gone through the day helping Mara with her duties at the nursing home. This woman who had not moved, had not changed so much as a facial expression the entire day, had captivated her from the moment she saw her lying on a gurney alone in the hallway, the morning sunlight spraying across her. Several different times throughout the day Clara had noticed her—always in a different place as she was being moved from room to room, floor to floor, testing, rehabilitating, the semblance of progression—each time somehow drawing Clara's attention no more completely than if she had sat up and yelled her name.

And now, as the day drew to a close, sitting in the chair beside the nightstand, Clara reached over and turned off the lamp.

So this is how it happens, she thought, looking into the eyes that see past today. *How can this happen? How could anyone let this happen to you?*

There in the dark.

"Was your life full? Did anyone love you?" she said, reaching out and gently taking the elderly lady's hand. The incidental sounds of movement came in under the door with a shaft of light, but otherwise it was quiet, temperate, and dark. Clara stood and leaned over the searching eyes, holding the bed railing with one hand for balance, nearly lying on top of her, face to face, peering in. She could feel breath lightly dust her cheek in shallow gusts. "Or were you alone?" she whispered. "How did you make it through, make it meaningful?" Still holding on to her hand, Clara lowered herself back into the chair and, without realizing it, dozed off.

*   *   *

The phone ringing early that morning, and not being answered, finally drove her out of bed and down the stairs. In the kitchen, she found Mara in a bathrobe, eating individually wrapped sponge cakes from a brightly colored cardboard box. Sitting there nodding her head along to the phone's insistent bell, and then seeing Clara, she sat back and waved a sponge cake toward the phone rattling away in its cradle.

"It's for you," she singsong said, her smile drifting sideways.

"Why don't you get an answering machine if you're not going to pick it up?" Clara huffed, a bit more than was necessary.

"Oh, well,' Mara responded, "let me see." She bopped her head back and forth, tapping the sponge cake on her lips like a soft, fat pencil. "My guess is," and she faux-brightened up, holding the sponge cake up with emphasis, and exclaimed cheerily, "it's your husband again, and, ahhh … he wants to know where the hell you're at and what the hell you're doing?" She batted big eyes at her sister. "How am I doing?"

76

"I'm sorry. I shouldn't have put it like that."

"Hmmmm." Mara narrowed her eyes and shoved in the sponge cake. Still chewing, she leaned forward. "Why don't you pick it up, and talk to him?" she said, simultaneously reaching again into the cardboard box.

Clara, looking at the growing pile of clear plastic individual wrappers on the table in front of Mara, changed the subject. "You have any coffee?"

"Sure. I think," she said, tearing open another sponge cake. "There was a jar of instant in the cupboard there, over the sink, if you want to put the kettle on," punctuating herself with another mouthful of preservative-laden goodness.

On her way to the sink, Clara reached out and pulled the phone jack from the wall. The ringing stopped.

"Ha!" exclaimed Mara, sitting back in her chair and pulling the cardboard box into her lap.

* * *

As the activities director at the nursing home, Mara's reputation was that of being efficient, patient, and caring. Everything a person could have hoped for, no more so than if concerned for a relative in the facility's care. Clara was impressed but not about to let on. She'd have never guessed based on their own dynamic that her sister could step out of herself like that and attend to the range of needs presented, one after another, all day long. She was pretty sure she didn't have it in her. Still, when Mara had asked if she wanted to go in with her and help out, almost absentmindedly, as a courtesy as much as anything, she'd surprised them both by accepting immediately.

Now, standing in the parking lot of the Green Pastures Nursing Home, smoking one last cigarette before going in (Mara had warned her about letting any of the residents see her cigarettes. "Some of them haven't been allowed to smoke since being placed here," she'd warned. "They'll murder you and hide your body if they sense they can get their hands on your pack."), she was having second thoughts. What did she know about elder care really? She'd been too busy with her own life, except maybe a weekend here or there, back when her parents could have used the help. It was, of course, Mara who'd done all the heavy lifting then, never forgetting to remind Clara that she'd regret it one day if she didn't get more involved.

That's two for Mara and zero for Clara, thought Clara.

Activities director, crossed her mind while stubbing out the filter and tossing it toward the receptacle. *What did that consist of? Making god's-eyes out of yarn and Popsicle sticks all day?* Still, being dismissive of her sister, in light of what she was doing in her own life, seemed more than a little contrite.

She opened the door and stepped into a warm humidity that smelled faintly of urine, disinfectant, and breakfast food. A sign was requesting politely but very firmly that anyone with a cold or virus refrain from going any farther. White linoleum floors, light green tiles on the wall capped with powder-yellow painted ceilings were in no way enhanced by the atrocious florescent lighting. Just inside the door was a sign-in book next to a basket of plastic flowers on an upright podium.

"Oooo," mouthed Clara looking at the somehow deliberateness of the arrangement. 'It's like the rehearsal for a funeral.'

All this plus the light olive green industrial clothing of the orderlies and the starched white-on-white of the nursing staff, bustling around in the hallways, in and out of doorways, you could, by not focusing on any one thing directly, have mistakenly thought you had entered a terrarium: a breeding ground for sponges and mushrooms tinged with the scent of hydrogen peroxide. As she stood there surveying the scene, the walls lined with wheelchairs whose occupants were in various stages of loss, all she could think of was that she could run now, ' ... *but it'll catch up to you eventually.*'

She found Mara organizing the morning television ritual for the first group out of the dining area; semicircle rows of wheelchair-bound faces, half of whom were staring at the floor. As cheering audience members egged on the game show contestants, the host overly pronouncing each scripted witticism between choreographed gambling for kitchen appliances, standing there Clara thought she might faint. For a moment it seemed as if a captive amphitheater of distressed helplessness was being mocked by a leisure-suited plastic surgeon for allowing themselves to become old and sick.

Mara, sensing what was happening, crossed the room and took Clara by the arm. "I think you and I need to talk," she said, leading her out through glass doors and into a garden area. Sitting down on a railroad-tie divider, Clara looked up at Mara.

"Yeah, go ahead, I guess," Mara said, looking back at the doors, "No one will see us out here, I suppose."

Clara fished the cigarettes and lighter out of her pocket.

"I know what you're thinking, and you better get it straight, okay?" Mara had turned her back and was running her hand through some flowering vines. "It is sad, pitiful even. You think I don't know that. Huh? I'm here every day." She turned back around, forcing Clara to face her.

"Do you know who these people are, sister, huh, do you? These are the parents of the people we went to school with, our teachers, the neighbors who looked out for us, everyone in this town." She stood up and looked over top of Clara.

"They're the people who remained behind, and the source of a bill that comes every month to those who left and can afford the luxury of not having to get their hands dirty, not have to invest in it."

Clara snapped to. "That didn't go over my head, Mara."

"Look, I saw you, okay. I know. I know you. But don't judge me, Clara, okay? Just don't. Don't look at me and judge what I'm doing here." She had begun moving, turning around on the flagstone path in front of Clara.

"These people, Clara, they have no one. Their families aren't going to swing by on their way home from vacation and pick them up. They're here to stay." She reached over and plucked the cigarette out of Clara's hand.

"They're here with me, with us," pointing with the cigarette back toward the doors. "Until they're not," and she drew on the cigarette, coughing.

"Christ, how can you smoke these things," she said, looking at the cigarette before dropping it on the stone and stepping on it, heading back toward the doorway.

* * *

Drifting awake, Clara wasn't sure how long she'd been sitting there, but on looking around, nothing seemed to have changed. It was late, and she'd been here since early that morning; the whole day. She stood to leave and saw that the old lady's eyes were closed. She made to step away and found that her hand was being held. She smiled at that and gently worked her way out.

* * *

"Thanks for waiting," Clara said as she came through the front door.

Mara was smiling at her over a brown paper Chinese food delivery bag. "Hey, you looked comfortable, so I figured I'd let you sleep it off and bring you breakfast in the morning." She was spooning in lo mein through a grin. "Want some?" she said holding up a dangling mass of brownish egg noodles.

Clara scrunched her nose up at the large oil spot seeping through the side of the bag. "I'm tired," she said, tossing her cigarettes onto the table in front of Mara. "Here, nothing says dessert like four or five of those before bed." She turned and began making her way to the stairs.

"Good niiiiight," sang Mara happily through a mouthful.

The irony wasn't lost on her, having only a short while ago witnessed the instant coffee, corn chip, and cake frosting breakfast, of now seeing Mara leading a group through stand-in-place aerobics. Clara stood on the other side of the window smoking, looking in and watching her sister hop about while her charges, at least those who appeared to be conscious of their surroundings, struggled to keep up with the raise-your-arms-now-lower-your-arms cheerleading. Wearing white socks, a one piece gray sweat suit and a blue terry cloth headband, Mara looked nothing short of a 1980s fitness instructor, albeit one who ate corn chips and cake frosting for breakfast. Still, one had to give credit where credit was due. After all, what had she done with her day so far? Besides chain smoking her way through a quarter of the pack she'd brought with her, and then hiding the stubbed-out butts under the bark mulch in the gardening, the answer was not much. Unless you counted lifting a certain someone's personal information folder out of the front office, and then the old girl herself, well then, that about made up her whole morning.

She walked back under the tree cover and sat down on a bench facing her self-appointed charge, who was seated in a wheelchair, pushed up off the trail so as not to be seen from the windows.

Was it a loss of recognition preceding a drift, or a clarifying recognition that prompted a turning away?

She'd been through the file, and one thing was certain: it didn't look like any resolutions would be forthcoming. How many drugs can one person take while under medical supervision? By the record in front of her here, apparently when it's a battle against mortality, the sky's the limit. What were all these prescriptions? Names she'd never heard of, let alone have been able to pronounce, poured down the page. Clara remembered taking some antihistamine as a little girl and how it knocked her for a loop. She could only guess at the heartbeat tidal-surge at work here. Could it be that she wasn't so much at the end of her rope as just stoned out of her mind?

Clara frowned—too easy; move on.

Old enough to precede the now de rigueur standard of recording every little personal detail, this was a life full of holes, on paper anyway: came to the town during the tail end of its heyday, made a career of teaching French in the public high school, never married, no children. One listed address, one work number, no emergency contacts. Clara had gone to that school and didn't remember any French classes. Of course, that didn't mean much. Anyone in this town who made the effort to learn French probably wasn't destined to hang around for long, things being as they were (are?) here. France. It all sounded dreamy, from a million miles away. *Parisian hair stylist* made her smile, and the realization that the phones in France never stop ringing either, brought her back to earth. This wasn't going to be a vacation.

So how does one become an enigma? There was no record of how mademoiselle arrived here, or even why she was here, although in her current state that was a question that pretty much answered itself. But it couldn't have just happened all of a sudden, could it? Had her history been lost to history?

"Isn't that," Clara then answered herself, "what happens to us all eventually?"

She closed the folder and rested her mouth on her fist, thinking that if it wasn't to be found on paper, then where did one find an answer? She looked over and considered that maybe you didn't find an answer, that it found you.

"When it caught up to you, were you ready?" she asked. She took out another cigarette and wondered what it was going to take for her. How would she know that she'd checked all her boxes? Was it too late to realize that which she hadn't considered? There was a feeling that she had been going along, living out the days like they model in television dramas, a social syndication awaiting those who followed quietly. Do you face it head-on, asking questions until they shut you up with a new prescription, or do you keep taking the prescriptions, a weariness willing to succumb?

It was getting hot, noon overhead, and she held the cigarette in her mouth, dug out her beaded barrette and clipped her hair back. With both hands supporting her head, she leaned back and exhaled the smoke through her lips, following the cloud with her eyes as it floated away … and into the teacher's face.

"Oops."

Standing to fan it away, she stopped herself just before noticing that her French instructor had very subtly drawn in through her nose, just slightly, barely perceptible, a bit of the dust.

"Ohhh, you're there," she leaned down and made direct eye contact, "aren't you?"

Clara remained there, crouched in front, her antenna up. Finally she took the cigarette out of her own mouth, turned it around in her hand and very gently placed it between chapped lips, and waited. A small red-crested bird landed in the tree above and began chirping frantically before Clara noticed the purplish-white blob drop through the leaves and onto the white cotton gown spread across the wheelchair.

"Who said that was good luck?" Clara murmured, pulling it toward herself for closer inspection. Folding it over to avoid explanation, she stood back and noticed the embers flare, heard the thin paper crackle. Her eyes widened, and a smile split her face as the smoke rose.

Life persists.

* * *

"Okay, if you're done with your petty thievery, kidnapping, and the shameful corruption of your elders," Mara was wiping her brow with her sleeve, "then I say we call it a day and get something to eat, I'm starving."

With that, Clara and her sister pseudo-Olivia Newton-John made their way across the road to a homogenous plastic restaurant serving ration-like pods of food. Mara ordered the Daily Double, where if the name alone didn't spell it out for you, the banner across the bag that should have read, 'Whatever doesn't kill you makes you stronger," would have. Clara sipped orange soda and picked the croutons out of a Styrofoam box full of brown lettuce.

Mara took the bun top off one of her burgers and held it out under Clara's nose. "If you're not going to eat that, then drop it on here."

Life persists.

We place a premium on life here and living it to the fullest, and yet," the nursing home orderly stated, "one can't work here for long before realizing that the old maxim holds true: death is persistent."

*   *   *

Clara had arrived to find the bed stripped of its cover and sheets, the thin mattress rolled up and balled, and an orderly rubbing down the metal frame with a bleach mix. She stood in the doorway to the room for a moment looking around while it sank in.

"The lady here, she is …," before trailing off.

The orderly, on her knees at the foot of the bed, stopped scrubbing long enough to size up Clara. "And you are?"

"Clara. My sister is Mara, the activities director here."

"Oh," she said, placing a hand on the frame and slumping forward a little. "Well, yes, I'm afraid to tell you that Ms. Bissette passed away sometime last night. She'd been taken to bed at lights out, and wasn't responsive this morning during medicinal rounds."

"I was just with her yesterday, and she seemed fine. I mean … a really good day actually."

Without looking up, the orderly shrugged, "We'll agree that she went out on a high note." She leaned back. "It was a happy ending then," she nodded. "We'll take it. Around here they're few and far between." With that she turned away and resumed her work.

"C'est la vie," she hummed under her breath.

"What's that?"

"C'est la vie." She looked up at Clara, "Such is life. It's French." And she again turned back to her work.

Clara walked over and sat down in the chair next to the bed. For a while she didn't say anything, just sat there while the orderly went about extinguishing any trace of a life from the area. After a bit, the orderly stopped again and turned to Clara. "You know, there was one thing, though."

"Yes," said Clara, frowning interest.

"Well," the orderly held the edge of the bed frame and used it to steady herself while standing. "It's probably nothing, you know, but the attending nurse who made the bed checks last night noted in her report that unlike every night she'd ever been assigned to that duty, last night Ms. Bissette's eyes were closed when she came through to check on everyone. She just thought it unusual is all." She shrugged her shoulders again.

Clara smiled thinking about that.

"And, oh yeah," the orderly said, twisting her face into a puzzle, "one more thing. The nurse also noted that she thought she smelled cigarette smoke."

Clara made ready to leave.

*　*　*

In the garden, she lit a cigarette and sat down on a bench. She wasn't going to get an answer, she feared, at least not here. Or if that was the answer—the puzzle is complete despite missing key pieces, specific answers—then it wasn't enough. For her it wasn't going to be enough to justify her actions, her anxiety. She felt a little sick to her stomach and closed her eyes, breathing slow and deep. She finished her smoke, stubbed it out, and tucked it under the bark mulch with her foot. At the doors, she stopped to read a flier posted on the glass:

Twenty-First Century Tulip Extravaganza— Overnight Field Trip

State Capital Convention Center

Sign up now at the Activities Desk or just ask Mara!

Really? thought Clara, *How come she wouldn't mention something like that to me?*

She'd find out, though, and on pulling open the door saw something in her reflection through the glass. Looking onto the shoulder of her blouse, there was a small purple and white blob. She immediately scanned the trees overhead but saw nothing, listened and heard nothing.

Still …

Good luck, huh? she thought. *Okay, we'll take it*, nodding to herself as she entered the building in search of the nearest bathroom. *Around here we'll take all we can get.*

Such is life indeed.

Stick 'em up!"

The chief, who'd been standing in the produce aisle steadily picking and eating fruit directly out of the bin, had thought he was alone, unseen. Turning around with his mouth full, a sliver of grape skin wedged between his two front teeth, he blushed slightly, adding color to his already ruddy forehead as he met Mara's wry smiling eyes.

"Ms. Kozlowski," he cleared his throat, covering his mouth with a fist. "How are you?"

Mara walked around her cart and, leaning in for a closer look, put a finger to the chief's mouth. "You've, ahhh, got something … stuck there, Chief," she got out, not quite suppressing a laugh.

"Oh, yes, well, ahhh, thank you," the chief said, working it now with his tongue, He stole a glance at the contents of Mara's cart.

What on earth?

"Hey, look, Chief while I have you here," and she leaned back, putting a hand on her hip. "If you have a minute, maybe you can do me a favor, huh?"

Swallowing and wiping his lips with a curled finger, the chief regained his composure and affected a mask of earnestness. "Well, I'll certainly try. What do you got?"

It looks like she's stocking a bomb shelter, for Christ's sake.

Mara again came around and stepped right into the chief's personal space, crowding his comfort zone and blocking him from being able to easily maneuver out of the way of her charm offensive.

"Well, as you may have guessed, over at the nursing home we're always looking for new ways to keep the residents active and on their toes. You know, keep them engaged."

"Hmmm, yes, I can imagine that's a full-time job," he said, frowning past her at the cart again.

What would one person possibly do with an entire case of whipped processed cheese in pressurized spray cans?

"So, anyway, this year," Mara was nearly bouncing in place now, "we've been considering taking some of the residents, those who are up to it, of course, over to the state capital for the annual tulip festival. We'd use the transport bus from the nursing home. I'd drive, and we'll spend the overnight in a local motel. Thing is …," and she rested a hand on the chief's fore-arm, "the home's operating director is a little concerned for the residents' safety and whether I could handle it alone. I'd need a little help, you know? Not so much a chaperone but a kind of guardian, you know? Lend an air of security, if you will. You know what I mean?"

"In other words," the chief was rocking back and forth on his heels now, arms folded, "you want me to take one of my men off the street and put him on your bus for a field trip with a bunch of grandmothers to a flower show? All on the taxpayers' dime, yes?"

Is that a wedding cake in there?

"Come on, Chief," Mara reached out and was clutching him now, making him uncomfortable, making him take notice. "These are the taxpayers, or their grandmothers, as you so eloquently put it." She'd narrowed her eyes at him, still holding on. "There must be someone you could spare for a couple of days, yes?"

Whoa, he thought, and the lights went on. Mara noticed and eased her grip, the corners of her lip curling up.

"Now that you mention it," the chief said, putting a finger next to his eye and massaging the faint bluish remnants. "I may have just the man you're looking for, yes." He looked off and smiled to himself.

Mara stepped back and clasped her hands in front of her. "That's wonderful, fantastic! I knew I could count on you to help us out."

The chief brought his gaze back into line with hers, and then tipping his head around to see behind her, let his smile dissolve into a look of concern as he noticed the small pool of clear liquid forming under Mara's cart.

Something's dripping?

"I'm not going anywhere with a bunch of old people, and that's that." Edna Little pursed her lips and nodded as if sealing the deal through a physical stamp of finality. She sat there in her wheelchair and waited for the inevitable response.

"Now, mother," Officer Nelson Little turned from the luggage he had laid out flat on the bed, "it's only for one night. They were nice enough to let me bring you along, so we'll be together, and it'll be fun."

"Fun," she scoffed. "Listening to a bunch of old whiners go on and on about their aches and pains, or worse, rattling on about their grandkids." She made that last one cut, knowing it never failed to get a rise out of her son.

Officer Little stood up straight and put his hands on his hips, looking down onto where his mother was sitting. "When was the last time you've gotten out of here, hmm?"

"Well, I was just up at the grocery—"

"Oh, come on, Mother, you know what I mean. It's not healthy. It's not good for you to stay in here cooped up all the time stewing over the television." He sat down on the edge of the bed so as to look at her directly. "Summer's almost over; it's cooling off a little at night now. Before you know it, it'll be snowing, and then your opportunity to get out and do something will have passed for another year. Besides," and he reached out to her, "when was the last time we got to do anything together? And you'll get to see me in action!" He was beaming.

Edna looked up. "Oh. Be still my beating heart," she said with a crooked smile, watching his deflate at the same time.

*   *   *

The chief took off his glasses, laid them on the nightstand, and climbed into bed. Lying there on his back in the dark, he exhaled loudly through his mouth and closed his eyes.

"Are you okay?" his wife replied from under the sheets next to him.

"Yes, yes, yes," he patted her back softly. "Just a long day, that's all." He opened his eyes and stared through the darkness at the ceiling. "There is one thing, though."

His wife turned over and propped herself up on an elbow. "Yes, what is it?"

"I've been thinking. You know that whatever happens, down the road or whatever ...," he was making his wife nervous now, anytime he started talking like this.

"Yes," she slowly let out, like any cop's wife would whenever these late-night talks reeking of "what if" arise.

"Well," he turned to her, and then away again, "no matter what, okay, no matter what, I don't ever want to go into that nursing home in town, okay?"

His wife smiled in the dark, put her head back onto the pillow, and closed her eyes. "Sure thing, Chief. Whatever you say."

It was pink lying there in her cart, a bone sharply protruding up against the plastic in which it was wrapped. What on god's green earth …?

He shuttered and tried to block it from his mind—tried to fall asleep.

The police cruiser's headlamps swept across the gravel parking lot, momentarily illuminating the group standing there. Circling around to pull alongside the other cruiser already parked there, Officer Nelson Little turned the wheel and, slowly crunching through the stones, brought the vehicle to a stop. He looked at the dashboard clock: four o'clock in the morning exactly. He looked over at his mother in the passenger seat next to him, her wheelchair folded into the backseat, their luggage in the trunk.

"Okay, here we are," he said. "Are you ready?"

She turned away slightly, looking at the floorboard. "Humph," registering a show of discontent with a quick shake of her head.

He let out a long, slow, and purposely loud fume of air from his mouth, only just feigning exasperation. She looked much smaller, frail even, strapped into the seat belt. She was outside of her element. It suddenly dawned on him that he'd need to be careful. He would need to look after her, keep her from losing herself in the situation, from feeling that she was unable to be in control of her own situation. It was an added responsibility that had not dawned on him until this moment. Outside it was still dark, and they were sitting there in the partial glow of an overhead street lamp. Refocusing his attention on the present, he realized that he'd been daydreaming and that she was looking at him, giving him a look that said, "I know what you're thinking, and don't." He reached over and took her hand in his; she looked at his hand and then narrowed her eyes at him.

"You're not wearing it. You brought it with you, right?"

"Yes," he said, withdrawing his hand. "I have it."

"Well, then put it on," she was adamant. "You can't keep going around with that stupid bread bag."

Through tightened lips he registered his disapproval. But then he reached into the backseat anyway and grabbed the green and yellow flowered oven mitt, slipping it over his damaged left hand before raising it up for her to see. He couldn't even look at it.

"There now," she exclaimed. "Isn't that better?"

He was frowning. "You're enjoying this, aren't you?"

"This better be good," she said, "or you're going to need to buy yourself a tent when we get back." She pulled her head down and looked up at him over her glasses.

"Ha!" he exclaimed. His mood turned on a dime. Twisting on his police cap with his one good hand, "This will be good," he laughed. Then, reaching across for the door handle, he smiled from ear to ear. "Let's get this ball rolling, shall we?" And he stepped out into the parking lot.

* * *

"Okay," the chief said, looking around at the group assembled next to the late model transport van, "looks like we're all here." He was staring at Officer Little's new cover as they walked up to where everyone was gathered.

"Hey, Little," he leaned over to within earshot, "what'd you do, get up early and bake cookies for the trip?"

"Hey, Chief," Edna said, pushing herself between the two police officers. "I think I saw a cat stuck in a tree on the way over here. Maybe you could be a hero and run over there, you know, and order someone else to take care of it." She pushed on through and began making her way toward the van without ever actually looking at him.

The chief watched her go, slowly shaking his head in her wake before turning back to the task at hand.

"Okay, Ms. Kozlowski ... Mara, this is Officer Nelson Little. He's going to travel with you folks and provide any assistance you may need. And over there," he said, motioning in the direction of where Edna was trying to force open the van door, "is his mother, Edna. Watch out for her, okay, Mara?" he said quietly. "If I know Edna it won't be long before she'll have pressured you into letting her drive or some such thing."

And with that, Mara made a quick round of introductions to acquaint everyone with each other: Mr. Henry Reinhardt, the twins Ms. Ruby and Ms. Rosie Rosenthal, and Miss Estelle Seybold, who between the four of them collectively accounted for some 320 years of experience.

"And, of course," Mara said, "that's my sister, Clara, who's coming along with us as well," the three of them turning toward her just in time to witness Clara grinding a cigarette butt into the gravel with her shoe. "You won't arrest her for littering, will you officer?" she said, laughing at Clara's embarrassment.

"Oh no, of course not," Officer Little responded, forcing himself to cease trying to recall the regulation regarding littering in a public area. "So this is it? It's a smaller group than I thought it would be."

"It's the first time we've done this, so it's a little new to everyone," Mara replied, now having noticed the oven mitt and finding it impossible to look at anything else. "We're hoping that this goes well, and we can do it again. Maybe then more residents will feel comfortable about wearing an oven mitt, I mean signing up." She blushed and looked sheepishly into Officer Little's face. "Sorry."

"Well, then, if that's it," the chief suggested, slapping Officer Little on the back, "then I say we load up and get you all on the road."

*   *   *

Clara, seated directly behind where Mara had sat down at the steering wheel, leaned in and whispered, "Are you sure you can drive this thing?"

"Watch this," Mara said, shifting the transmission out of park and giving it enough gas to spin the rear wheels in the gravel. Until, that is, the van scraped up to a stop alongside the chief's patrol car, creasing in his passenger side door panel with a loud metallic crumpling.

"Oops," Mara said, covering her mouth with her hand as she saw the chief, who'd had to jump out of the way, curse through clenched teeth in the rearview mirror.

"Excuse me," Officer Little called out from his seat near the back of the van, "But I think there's been an accident." He was looking out the window to where Mara had backed into the patrol car.

"No, no, I think we're okay," Mara responded, guiltily glancing at Clara as she turned back toward the windshield. She shifted the transmission from reverse into drive and began pulling out onto the road. "I think we're good."

The chief stood there watching them go, shaking his head as the transport van, with one of its now broken and no longer functioning taillights, disappeared into the darkness. He made his way over to his patrol cruiser, pulling open the driver's side door and, while still looking in the direction of where the transport van had gone, slipped in the gravel, smacking his forehead against the door frame before falling into the seat behind the steering wheel.

"*Oooooooohh*," he blew as his hand reached up and pressed against the rapid swelling. He watched in the rearview mirror as the purple tint bubbled over his eye as it slowly closed under the now throbbing bulge.

"Jesus H. Christ," he muttered to himself as he dropped back onto the seat.

As it was, with her back to the window, legs up and stretched out straight along the bench, she could just see over the back of her seat, able to look across at the other passengers, the strangers she was riding with, unobserved from the shadows.

She closed her eyes and was flying.

Floating through an endless blue-black sea of air, under a million stars, she let it all fall away. Looking down at the tiny light-sprinkled globe where her concerns had seemed paramount, seeing it slide by underneath, she let it all peel off, fold over and back, drop free, and disappear out of sight. She held her arms straight back, pressed them tight to her sides, held her breath and began to increase her speed. She stiffened her neck, tipped her head up slightly, and began gaining altitude.

Something was beside her.

Something that she couldn't see, something that she was afraid to look at, was beside her, keeping pace. The wind was buffeting on her face. She opened her eyes, and they watered. A single drop ran across her cheek, down her neck and torso, slid the length of her leg, curving onto her foot, out to the end of her toe where it hung for just a moment—and then broke free. She turned her head slightly. The air swam though the channels in her ears, flowing in and out smoothly, streamlining, and it became quiet. She felt peaceful enough to again close her eyes and just … feel. Feel the air, feel the sensation of thoughts evaporate, and a clarity of space unfolded in her mind. It was right there. She could sense it.

"*I have to pee.*"

It was the first small crack in the ice covering a pond. A splintering that spread. She slowed and descended.

"Hey, Clara." She knew that voice. "Clara, wake up."

Her eyes opened slowly, from a fog, staring. Soft-focus vision of her hand in front, an involuntary slow-motion reflex of release, and the coffee thermos she'd been holding tipped over and drained its contents across the seat, soaking her legs in the lukewarm liquid. She breathed it in, and began to doze away.

"Clara!" Mara was twisting her head back. "Hey, Clara, wake up, huh! What are you doing?"

She snapped out of it, startled, and immediately jumped to see if she was being watched, embarrassed. Nothing, and yet …

The sun was up, and everything was different, looked different. There was a flurry of activity midway back through the rows of seats, and she squinted, focusing on the single lady, the one who had gotten on alone. As she looked to her, she was in turn being looked at, directly, from across the aisle.

"I had to pee," explained Miss Seybold with sad eyes and a smile.

The old guy, Henry what-ever-his-name-was was there, and the cop. They were bent over, cleaning apparently. Clara watched through the gauze-filter of waking as the cop ran his hand back and forth across the bench, back and forth with his ridiculous oven mitt. Finally, after an unspoken agreement between the two, the thoroughness of the work the best that could be done under the circumstances, the cop pulled out a bread bag from his pocket and dropped in the sopping mitt.

Clara turned to first see Mara's eyes reflected in the rearview mirror, observing, and then saw them drop and register something else altogether.

"Oh, Jesus Christ!" Mara shouted, nearly standing up and using both feet to stomp on the brake pedal; she held the steering wheel with both hands and physically tried to pull the entire transport van back from the traffic that had come to a stop in the middle of the road. Everyone leaned forward into the skid, except Clara, who rolled off the bench onto her back on the floor, and the cop, who took a big, flat-footed step forward, slapping his shoe down loud and, like a pitcher releasing a fastball, sent the bread bag and its contents airborne, up through the vehicle where it hit the inside of the windshield wet, stuck for a moment, and then slid down onto the dashboard.

Eeeeeeww, Clara thought, feeling the van break sideways slightly, sliding through a black cloud of smoldering tires, to a stop just short of the bumper ahead. From her vantage point on the floor, she watched Mara exhale and slowly lay down face first onto the steering wheel, still clutching it with both hands.

Yeah, I know what you're thinking," said old Henry, looking across at Clara, "and you're right—getting old sucks!"

*　*　*

They were all feeling better now that they'd had a chance to get out, clean up, stretch, whatever, at the gas station. Between the little accident with Miss Seybold in the seat and the very nearly enormous accident out there on the road, things had started to fray slightly, and Mara deemed it wise to pull over and regroup.

Edna Little had stayed on the van, plying a caustic eye on the diorama unfolding around her. Miss Seybold, now obviously free of any inner tensions, slumped soundly against her seat, eyes closed and smiling in the sunshine. The twins, radiating effervescence in a better world of their own making, stood side by side and waved to the passing traffic on the highway going past.

Clara stepped out of the van and past old Henry, who had stationed himself just outside the door. She walked a few feet forward, stopped, and lit a cigarette and, while breathing it in, thought better of turning to meet his stare that she knew was waiting behind her. She gave it a minute and then, just when she sensed he was preparing to say something to her, walked on to the station, absentmindedly flicking her cigarette out toward the gas pumps before pulling open the doors and stepping in.

The cop was already there, searching through the aisles for something. When he saw her, he stood up straight, smiled ear to ear, and waved to her with his unraveling bandaged hand. She smiled back and lifted a hand in his direction. Through the window, far enough back that she herself couldn't be noticed, she watched as old Henry wandered over to where she'd tossed her cigarette in the parking lot, picked it up, and walked off with it in his mouth.

She walked over to the first counter she came to, grabbed a box of antibacterial sanitary hand-wipes and held them up so the kid with the glass eye behind the counter could see.

"I'm going to buy these," she pronounced. "Have you got a restroom in here?"

The kid directed his eye toward the back of the store, and she followed suit, opening the door to the small unisex toilet and then locking herself in. Tearing off the top of the box, she pulled open and then dropped on the floor a cardboard square. Kicking off her shoes one at a time, she then stood on the square before pulling her pants off, folding them over and placing them on the porcelain sink's lip. Pulling out a handful of the lemony-smelling towels, the aroma counter-balancing nicely with the dried coffee, she proceeded to wipe down her legs. No surprise, there didn't appear to be any hand towels in the restroom. So she slowly blew down onto her legs until she felt them dry and then got dressed.

* * *

Back on the road, with the sun streaming through the windows, there really wasn't any way to avoid confronting each other at this point. Clara looked around. With Mara revitalized behind the wheel, full of renewed confidence behind her new cheap gas station sunglasses and fortified with an extra-large bag of freeze-dried onion rings ("Just like the astronauts eat!"), they appeared to once again be in good hands. She watched the cop as he slowly rewrapped what was left of his hand in a bandanna he'd bought at the gas station.

"Hey."

Clara looked over and saw old Henry leaning toward her from across the aisle.

"You ever seen that commercial on TV, the one with the well dressed, smiling old couple who say that you can get your incontinence supplies delivered discreetly to your door? So you can get on with your life? And they look and act like it's the greatest thing to happen to 'em ever? You ever seen that commercial on TV?"

Clara frowned slightly and nodded no.

"Well, don't believe it. Take it from me," he said pointing a finger at her, "that's bullshit. 'Get on with your life' my ass." He shook his head with genuine disgust. "The time to get on with your life is when you're young, like you." He was pointing at Clara again. "No one wants to visit the pyramids wearing a diaper."

"Henry Reinhardt. Why don't you leave that girl alone?"

Old Henry turned and looked back to where Edna Little was sitting.

"I remember you, Edna Little," he said. "You're a hard woman."

"Ha!" laughed Edna, "I remember you too, Henry Reinhardt. I remember that time you pinched me in the grocery store, and I remember that a week later my husband got drunk and kicked your ass in the parking lot outside the county fairgrounds." Genuine satisfaction was in her tone.

Old Henry glowered at her from across the transport van. "You're a hard woman, Edna Little." He stewed for a moment before turning back to Clara.

"Hey. I read a story one time. That daredevil guy, Evel Knievel, took a red, white, and blue motorcycle over to Europe, gonna jump over a bunch of buses. The night before, he stayed up late drinking in a hotel room full of women, telling everyone who would listen that he wasn't gonna make it. He could feel it was going wrong." He was looking over at Clara with real seriousness in his eyes. "Do you know what he did?"

Clara was listening, shaking her head no.

"Well, you know, he got up the next morning, climbed on that motorcycle just like he said he would, and hit that landing ramp at one hundred miles an hour, cartwheeling over the handlebars and flying out onto the field; failing spectacularly!" He was smiling to himself now.

"Hey, I got another one." He was pointing at Clara again.

"Frank Morris. Do you know who he is? No? Well this guy escaped from Alcatraz prison. That's right." He narrowed his eyes to impart resonance, "Alcatraz, the big house. Do you know they looked for him for years, followed all kinds of leads from all over the country, and turned up nothing? That would be the end of it there, I guess, except you know what?"

Clara did not.

"Every now and then someone mentions that they ran into him somewhere. He's menacing some housewife and her kid in a department store, telling them his name like it's supposed to mean something. Ha! Crazy." Old Henry sat there smiling and nodding to himself.

"Hey, Henry," Edna called from the back of the van, "I got one for you, okay?" Henry hesitated in turning to meet Edna's eye. "These stories of yours, do they have a point, or are you just pulling leaves off the Alzheimer's tree?"

Old Henry gritted his teeth and dropped his head. Without looking up, he said, "You wouldn't know, Edna, would you, living at home with your son." He was staring out the window now, nodding.

He turned around and looked straight at Clara.

"I have a son. I worked my whole life, did just what they said to do: keep a steady job, raise a family, and pay all my taxes. Lived between the lines. And you know what that got me?" he said to Clara. "Hey, you know what that got me, Edna," turning back to look at her, "do you? I was breathing those fumes at the mill, I got ... I don't know," he shook his head in confusion, "I got ... tired or something. Damn it. And my boy, my son, he thought the best thing for me would be to go into that home so I could get the care I need; that's what he said, so I could get the care I need."

Everyone was quiet, watching old Henry wrestle with his life—watching for anything they might be able to use in their own private battles.

"So, yeah, now when I read about these nuts that went their own way, crashed and burned on their own time, I think about it differently now—the fun they must have had, living their lives, living with a capital L ... throwing it all away like that. Oh yeah ...," he trailed off for a moment. "So now I don't miss anything." He stood up and looked right at Edna. "I've watched all the damn television I ever want to watch, no offense, Mara," he said, acknowledging her in the rearview mirror. "But when they said there was going to be a trip to a tulip festival, in the state capital? Well sign me up, every time. Hell, I'll be honest, at this point I'd ride along to a casket maker's convention if it'd get me out in the mix even just one more time."

All the passengers in the van were slowly nodding now, including Edna.

Clara could tell when Mara was thinking, and even behind her sunglasses, yeah, Mara was thinking. Everyone had turned inward except the cop. Clara peeked at him over her seat, and he was sitting straight up, looking directly at old Henry. At first Clara thought maybe he was mad at how Henry had spoken to his mother. But after watching for a couple of minutes, she didn't think so. It was different, like he was trying to figure something out. *Like he wanted ... to do what*, Clara thought, *help?*

"Hey."

Clara turned back, and again old Henry was leaning across toward her, pointing a slightly shaking finger at her.

"Hey, I got something else, my favorite, okay?"

He was smiling broadly now; the sun was shining right onto him, and with each passing moment he seemed to be gaining strength from it. "I knew this girl, this tough girl, you know, and do you know what she used to do, huh?"

Clara did not know.

"Well," he said, happily laughing under his breath, "do you know she would squirt Grey Poupon mustard onto Pringles potato chips and then sit and eat the whole container. Crazy."

Clara looked on as Henry closed his eyes and sat back into the sunshine, watching his tough girl eat through another container of chips. She reached into her pocket and tossed a new pack of cigarettes and a book of matches across the aisle and onto the seat next to him.

Somewhere half a world away, the sick and crippled pilgrims were climbing into streams of healing water, descending into a necropolis's refrigerated revisionism, stumbling around in the desert's dizzying vortex. Into churches, temples, mosques, and monasteries they poured on their knees, spilling tears under the spell of a thousand promises, in a thousand languages from a thousand books; shuddering on their backs under the witch doctor's dead chicken.

Over here, the shuffling elderly masses were making their way across the great asphalt expanse. Perhaps one last opportunity to see the bulbs being planted, and not *be* the bulbs being planted. The Twenty-First Century Tulip Extravaganza was under way, and from the windows in the transport van, as they pulled off the roadway and into the parking lot, it looked like Ponce de Leon's worst nightmare: the lure of a fountain of youth turned radically on its head—advertising-induced hypnosis masking a commode of disposal.

With the engine still idling, Mara brought the van to a stop. Immediately the car behind began blowing its horn in long, incremental, piercing blasts. Peering into the rearview mirror to see, she could make out the car's quartet of occupants: pinched hatchet-faces, their old veined eyes cursing her through the glass. Snorting, Mara grabbed the wheel, swung the transport van out of the traffic lane and into a parking slot, pulling in and hitting a light pole. For a moment, with the sound of the impact still in the air, the pole teetered, before the lamp dropped out, falling to the ground, shattering and spraying shards of glass over the immediate area.

"Well," she said, beaming, "we made it."

Everyone remained quietly in their seats as they watched an old lady with a walker slowly make her way through the carpet of crystal chips and over to the driver's side window.

"I saw that, young lady," she directed toward Mara. "That was your fault. You better call the police and report it."

Mara leaned out the window, hitched her thumb toward the back of the transport van, and coolly intoned, "No problem. We brought our own cop." She smiled, and her new gas-station sunglasses slipped off her face and fell to the ground, breaking. "Oh, goddamn it, will you look at that?"

The old lady drew in her breath with a theatrical sense of disapproval before turning away and shuffling off.

The acres of asphalt parking spaces spread out under the sun, the grid strategically punctuated by gun-metal gray light poles, giving the appearance of steel plants erupting from a black earth—hell's own inedible garden. All this anchored by an enormous concrete box with entrances on its four soulless sides. Echoing shades of some medieval idolatry, the only thing missing were priests' bleeding Christ figures on lawn chairs out front. One couldn't help but notice that there seemed to be an awful lot of transport vans parked there.

"Okay, I'm just going to say it," said Edna, "Am I the only one who feels like we've just arrived at the world's largest nursing home?" She was staring at the long line of ambulances parked next to the Convention Center.

"It's, it's like … the mothership," said Henry in a daze, watching row after row of his peers disappearing into the entrances. "Kind of reminds me of those boxes you'd set out on your kitchen floor to draw in the roaches."

Mara was standing up now and looking down the aisle with her hands spread out in front of her. "Okay, come on, what is wrong with you people, huh? This is going to be fun."

No one seemed convinced.

"Look, all right," she was selling it now, animated. "We're going to go in here and check this out, okay? And if it sucks," at which point she looked directly at old Henry, "then we leave. No big deal. I've got us rooms for the night at the motor-lodge motel just down the street, and there are a whole slew of restaurants we can choose from for dinner tonight. It's going to be fun, right?" and she threw her arms up in a sign of triumph.

"Hey."

Everyone looked over at where old Henry had left his seat and was now pressing his hands flat against the windows.

"Over there," he was saying, staring across the road. "Is that … is that …" His face was now almost flat against the window. "Is that what I think it is?"

"What are you talking about, Henry," Mara replied, "huh?"

Everyone on the transport van now moved to the side where old Henry was glued to the window, searching the near-distant horizon for the source of his reverence.

"Mother of God," old Henry whispered. "It … it is." He stood back and pointed across the street. "Look!" he shouted.

It took a moment, but soon Clara and Mara and Nelson and Edna and Ruby and Rosie and Estelle all zeroed in on it as well. In the sunlight it was harder to make out, but with prolonged effort the vision clarified itself, the electric lights burning a beacon for all to see.

The Cow Palace Casino & Resort stood like a dethroned empress out slumming among her shabby subjects.

"Mara," Henry said, "start the van."

"Ah, no," said Mara. "We're going to the Tulip Festival, just like we planned, and then we're going to the motel and have dinner, and then in the morning we're driving back home." She folded her arms across in front of her. "We are most certainly not," again looking directly at old Henry, "going to the, what is it, the Cow Palace Casino & Resort? No way, Henry."

"Please, Mara," Henry said, "This is our moment; this could be it, huh?" He started gesturing with his arms. "This is where we jump the buses, yeah? This is where we escape from the island." He went back to the window and pressed himself up against the glass. "Just look at it over there." He was at this point talking to himself as much as to anyone else, "Just look at it, will you?"

*   *   *

Clara, on her knees in the bench behind the driver's seat, leaned forward and reached over, wrapping both her arms around Mara's chest and resting her chin on her sister's shoulder as they both looked through the windshield at the crowd outside the entrance to the Cow Palace Casino & Resort.

The entrance itself was a low-slung affair, rimmed with pink and yellow lights and shading the large vehicular turnaround from the sun. Outside the tall gilded doors was a line of what appeared to be security staff, well-dressed, broad-shouldered, serious men giving off an air of little humor, each one routinely reaching up and touching the small wired bulb lodged in their left ears, listening intently and glancing around through dark sunglasses. Across from them, behind a roped-off partition keeping them at a respectable distance from the entrance, was an altogether different breed of men: middle-age, middle-brow, middle-class men who also apparently shared the same fashion sense. They looked agitated, heated, and confrontational. They carried sandwich boards and placards with sayings such as, "Sinning Is Not Winning" and "Don't Royal Flush Your Life Away." One of them had an electronic megaphone and was preaching a gospel of piety, fire, and brimstone.

"Oh no," said Mara, surveying the scene.

"Looks like we got here just in time for the clash of civilizations," remarked Clara. She poked Mara in the back and started laughing. "You know, this might be good."

Mara looked at her with eyes of disbelief. "When did I become the responsible sister?"

"Don't worry," replied Clara, not looking at her and keeping a watch on the scene unfolding out front, "you're not."

"What I want to know is," called out Edna from the back of the transport van, "where are all the women? Every time I see these moralists on the news it's always the same bunch of angry white guys. I mean, it's the middle of the afternoon. Don't these people have jobs?" She was taking them apart through the window with her eyes, one by one.

"Bah," scoffed old Henry in response, "these are the losers who didn't believe in condoms, got their first girlfriends pregnant, and now they're trying to narrow everyone else's possibilities." He was busy giving the finger to as many as would look up at him as possible. "Tomorrow they'll be out firebombing an abortion clinic or up at the statehouse trying to revoke someone else's citizenship."

Mara stood and, with her hands on her hips, turned toward everyone in the van. "I don't know. Maybe we better just go back over to the Convention Center like we originally planned."

The sense of gloom that immediately descended over the transport van was as if all oxygen had suddenly been siphoned off; mouths opened, but nothing was said. Clara tried to stifle her laugh, but ended up only snorting it into her clenched fists, ducking her head away from Mara as a last resort.

Exasperated, Mara bent down next to Clara. "You know you're not helping, right?" Clara couldn't help it and squashed another one out, heaving slightly on her bench seat.

"Look!" old Henry was pointing out into the parking lot, "It's a warrior for the cause!"

Everyone turned and watched as the pair strode closer into view. He in a wide-lapel powder-blue suit, white leather shoes and belt, crew cut high-and-tight; she on black leather knee-high heels, fleshy with raccoon eye shadow and a Clorox beehive.

"Man look at that," said Henry. He turned and steadied a finger at Clara. "You can only get away with that if you're *living* your life." For a moment Clara thought he might need to sit down.

The couple strode alongside the transport van on their way to the casino's entrance doors, stopping when they noticed the twins waving to them through the windows. Aphrodite blew them a kiss and clung onto Hercules's arm, he who looked up, nodded acknowledgment, and dipped a small bow to them before continuing on. Striding by the moralists, the couple exuded an almost visual sense of empowerment as they made their way past: without judgment, insecurity, or concession. For the protestors' part, seeing the living, breathing embodiment of everything they seemingly didn't understand, lacked personal experience of, and perhaps even harbored a repressed desire for, those without sandwich board shields turned away and projected their internal contradictions into the mirror of one another.

"Excuse me, Ms. Kozlowski," Officer Nelson Little said as he came up alongside Mara, "and Ms. Kozlowski," he looked to Clara and pulled his policeman's cap farther down on his brow, "but I think maybe this is where I can be of some assistance."

Okay, hold on a moment," Clara said, stepping back to get a better look at the sisters. Even at their advanced age, the Rosenthal twins remained remarkably similar. Of course, this was aided by the fact that they dressed and made each other up as they would themselves: Ruby being Rosie's mirror and vice versa. They weren't big talkers, but when it became apparent that it was going to be table games and not tulips, they had set into action, preparing for a change in the weather, so to speak. As Clara had watched them bustling about in their seat, digging through the tote bag they'd brought and pulling out makeup compacts and small jars of creameries, it dawned on her that maybe this wasn't the first time the twins had been under a roof of indulgences.

Nodding her approval at the red shoes, red lips, and red scarves wrapped around their china-white sun dresses and necks, Clara put her hands on her hips. "Give us a smile."

The sisters' faces lit up simultaneously as they widened their mouths. "Oh," Clara exclaimed, "wait a minute." She licked her forefinger and pushed it between Ruby's lips, brushing the red lipstick smear off her yellow front teeth. "There," she said, putting one hand each on the twins' knees. "You both look beautiful." They in turn each put a hand on top of hers and became luminous.

"Hey, look," called out old Henry, "here comes Do-Right."

Everyone turned and watched as Officer Nelson Little came out through the casino's doors. Stiff as a board, he walked straight up between the opposing groups of assembled men. The police uniform imparting a respect that he flew like a flag on the battlefield, he stopped halfway between where the transport van was parked and the entrance to the Cow Palace Casino & Resort.

"Ha," old Henry laughed. "That boy of yours is something else, Edna."

"One more crack like that," Edna shot back, "and I'll have him handcuff you to your seat, you old fool."

After several times looking back and forth to assess the situation, Officer Nelson Little then looked across at Mara and gave her a thumbs-up. When she made a move toward exiting the transport van, though, he held up his hand, imparting her to stop.

Still holding out his wrapped and bandaged hand, he looked back over toward the line of security staff and gave them a nod. As two of the guards stepped around and pulled open the entrance doors, Officer Nelson Little began to windmill his other arm in a fashion that bespoke the direction of traffic.

A collective gasp went up in the transport van as the first in the line of five candy-apple-red electric motorized scooters pulled out single-file through the doors. Each driven by a gold and white sheathed member of the valet staff, they floated past Officer Nelson Little, between the two opposing cultural armies, and pulled up alongside the transport van.

Mara opened the door just as the head valet walked up to the van.

"Ladies and gentleman," said the valet, laying an arm across the front of his chest and spreading the other out toward the motorized scooters, "Welcome, to the Cow Palace Casino & Resort."

*   *   *

"You know," said Mara, coming up behind Clara just inside the casino's foyer, "if anyone back at the nursing home hears about this, I'll be lucky if I still have a job changing out catheters."

Nothing says "preferred customer" quite like five disposable incomes let loose in a hedonistic playground. And Edna, Estelle, Ruby, Rosie, and Henry were getting it in spades. In their complimentary scooters, free drinks in hand and being led across the room by no less than three peacock-feathered showgirls, the last Clara saw of them they were parading their way deeper into everything denied upstanding members of neighborhood watch groups, parent-teacher associations, and church basement potluck dinners.

"Well, when in Rome I guess," and Mara threw her hands up in the air. "You know, I was thinking that maybe we won't have to say anything about …," and she stopped talking long enough to draw Clara's attention back to her. "Hold on." Mara had pushed past Clara now and was staring into an adjacent room at the bottom of a small set of stairs off to one side. "Holy shit!" she exclaimed, involuntarily pulling and snapping at the waistband on her sweatpants. "Holy shit! I've heard about these, but I never thought I'd actually see one. Look," she pointed, turning to face Clara, "it's one of those all-you-can-eat casino buffets!"

Clara looked at Mara instead.

"Oh, come on, Clara," she said, tugging at her pants. "Let's go, huh?"

Looking more out of place than at any time since they'd been in each other's proximity, Clara noticed Officer Nelson Little making his way through the crowd, watching and, equally so, being watched by the carousers around him. He noticed the Kozlowski sisters, waving to Clara, and began making his way over.

"Okay, whatever." Mara spun Clara around and, holding her by both shoulders, looked directly into her face. "I will not be denied this indulgence." And she began making her way over to the room of steaming trays.

"Think of all the starving children in Africa," Clara called after her. Mara held up her middle finger without looking back. Smiling, Clara watched her go, and then saw her reach out and grab Officer Nelson Little just as he was approaching.

"Hey, Law & Order," Mara yelled over the din, tightly holding onto his arm. "I'm going over here and clean them out of king crab legs. And you," she looked up into his semibewildered eyes, "are going to have my back, make sure I'm not sexually assaulted by any mob bosses or card sharks, got it?" Pulling him along behind her, he had just enough time to quickly look over at Clara with a questioning glance before they both disappeared behind the serving tables.

*   *   *

They had everything you could want, given, that is, you know what it is that you want. Clara was beginning to think that the reason she couldn't formulate an answer was because she'd never actually had a question. But the resolution to her non-question still demanded an answer. *You're not out here to fill in gaps in the past*, she thought. *You're seeing if it's too late to build a future that may not even exist for you.* She sat down at one of the tables on the low balcony overlooking the gaming floor and pulled the cigarettes out of her purse.

"Can I get you a drink, honey bun?"

Clara looked up at the roving waitress with the pillbox hat and the cigar-box-on-straps at her waist. "Umm, something cold," she shrugged.

"Yeah, okay, sure." The waitress smiled and laid down a paper doily on the table in front of her. "I'll be right back."

Clara lit the cigarette, cleared her mind, and just smoked, slowly blowing the dust out. After she'd gone several minutes lost in the process, she looked over the railing and began scanning the tables below her. *Oh, boy*, she thought on seeing old Henry, with Rosie on one side of him and Ruby on the other, Estelle and Edna looking on, lined up at one of the card tables. Henry was pushing out chips onto the table, and the dealer was laying out cards.

"Here you go doll," and the waitress set down a small green glass tumbler full of ice and a clear liquid. "Take it easy, okay? It's from Russia and starts with a *v*." She winked at Clara and began heading off. "I'll check back on you in a little bit."

A crowd cheering from below drew her attention back to the tables, and, taking her drink in both hands, she looked just in time to see old Henry reach out and pull back toward him and the twins a whole pile of chips. People in the growing crowd behind them were leaning over to one another and speaking behind cupped hands. She strained to see closer. *What the hell?* she thought on seeing that Henry had two lit cigarettes in his mouth at the same time. The crowd became silent. She watched the five of them huddle below her from their motorized scooters, leaning across the table. Finally they all five sat back, and Henry looked to each before speaking.

"Okay, Miss Seybold," he said looking at Estelle first, and then turning to the dealer. "We're all in," and he pushed the entire pile of chips out onto the table with both hands.

The crowd erupted in cheers around them.

A girl in a black velour bikini walked across the tabletop and swung around to stand there over the players. Clara watched as Henry, sitting back in his motorized scooter and looking up, spotted her in the balcony overhead.

"Clara Kozlowski!" he shouted, pointing at her. "We're all in, Clara!"

Clara took a sip of the drink, put her cigarette in her mouth, crossed the fingers on both her hands, and with her arms straight out on the table in front of her, closed her eyes after seeing the dealer slide a single card out of the boot, face down on the tabletop.

"You hear that, Clara!" They were shouting up from the tables.

"We're all in, Clara; we're letting it ride!"

Mara practically stumbled over to where Clara was waiting at the casino's exit doors, still with Officer Nelson Little in tow. He remained a step behind her, monitoring the facial expressions of those Mara was pushing out of her way. When she finally made it over, she grabbed Clara with one hand and, bending over at the waist, exhaled as if she'd just completed her portion of an Olympic triathlon.

"Whew," Mara said, standing up straight and throwing her head back, hands on her hips. "That was something."

Clara lit a cigarette and watched as her sister caught her breath. "So you found the others? They're coming?"

"Oh yeah," she said, still trying to modulate her breathing, "they're over there." She was pointing across the foyer. "The concierge is buttering them up and giving them vouchers for the next best time of their lives—it'll be a wonder if any one of them doesn't end up deciding to stay, and then we'll end up having to use Officer Brute Force here," she said looking to Officer Little, "to get them back on the transport van."

Clara smiled as she saw Officer Nelson Little, not having heard what was just said, reach out and clothesline a tipsy patron with his arm, only steps and seconds from where he'd have crashed into an unbeknownst Mara from behind. Clara gazed through the smoke as she watched Officer Nelson Little take the inattentive pedestrian and steady him with a smile and a hand on each shoulder; the pedestrian sobered with a "what's-a-cop-doing-in-here?" look on his face as he hurried away into the bustle.

"Come on." Mara waved her arm through the air. "You two wait over here. I told them we'd pull the transport van around to the front doors and pick everyone up there."

*   *   *

"So, Officer Little," Clara said, pleasantly needling him with her eyes through the cigarette smoke. "Did you and my sister have a nice dinner together?"

Officer Nelson Little fought through the awkwardness he brought to every casual conversation to stammer out, "Your sister does not lack tenacity."

He's blushing, thought Clara, dipping around slightly and squinting, trying to regain eye contact. *Here's an odd one*, she said to herself, standing there looking directly up at him. He stood there unmoving, frozen in place, and now staring directly across the road in front of the casino. Putting a hand up in front of his face, nothing? She turned, stood on tiptoes and shoulder to shoulder now, tried to make out what it was that had so drawn him away from her.

Clara saw a chain-franchised family restaurant, buttressed by yet another chain-franchised family restaurant, the monotony broken only by the inclusion of a chain-franchised sports bar. In fact, she thought it looked like damn near every chain-franchised restaurant in the entire country had an out-post across the street. Still ... she looked back at Officer Nelson Little, who hadn't moved, and then back across the street.

It was the balloon that first caught her attention.

One, then another, and soon ... hundreds, maybe? She frowned and followed their trajectory back to the point of origin, which revealed itself to be a fanning-out across the parking lot of screaming children in party hats, intermingled with distressed parents waving their arms in the air. *What kind of parent would throw his or her kid a birthday party where ...,* she was in the process of thinking when the door to Chuck E Cheese flew open, the piercing ring of bells cut through the air, and a giant mouse ran through the doorway and out into the parking lot.

Clara's mouth dropped open. She pointed across the street. "The other night ... in a motel ... on the television ...," she was saying as she turned to look at Officer Nelson Little.

He was standing already facing her, when he reached out and held her by the shoulders. "Clara, I'm going to need you to get everyone inside, now!" He then turned and began galloping off like a limping camel toward the chaos. She watched him go, stunned for a moment, staring at him receding, and then at his bandaged hand, tattering along beside him, when the pieces began to fall together for her.

"Oh, no, no, this can't be happening," she was saying aloud just as Mara pulled up in front of her in the transport van.

"What's up with Magnum Force?" Mara said, leaning out the window. "I mean, if he's still hungry, he could have waited for us, huh?" She was shaking her head looking at him running toward the street. "We could have all gone over together."

*   *   *

The giant mouse, a gun in one hand and a canvas sack in the other, was the first one to reach the street, quickly looking both ways before running out between a break in the traffic. Officer Nelson Little, huffing, puffing, sweat pouring into his eyes, never even slowed to look, just simply caterwauled straight out into the roadway from the other side, slamming directly into his nemesis. The giant mouse went down backward onto his carpeted butt in the street; Officer Nelson Little, like some crazed member of a ballet troupe, spun and pirouetted, throwing his hands up, before toppling over sideways onto the blacktop. The canvas sack burst open, and a giant green flower bloomed in the air over them as both cop and robber regained their footing. For a moment they stood and stared at each other: the cop at the mouse's gun, the mouse at the cop's damaged hand, and then it became real again.

"*Aaaaahhhhhhhhhh,*" Officer Nelson Little let out his war cry and charged, arms flailing widely, whereby he both knocked the gun out of the giant mouse's hand, and managed to trip over his own feet and go down hard, face-first. Looking down at where the cop had fallen, even through the dense layer of carpeted disguise, the giant mouse managed to impart a sense of "This couldn't be the same cop, could it?" before bending down to retrieve his gun. Checking to see that it was still serviceable, the giant mouse then looked up ...

And into the face of Clara Kozlowski.

Standing there looking at one another, Clara came up level to the giant mouse's chest. The giant mouse spread his arms apart as if to give a hug, and a muffled voice filtered out through the fur, "You got to be kidding."

Clara reached into her purse, pulled out her Home Shopping Network Taser and, jamming it between the giant mouse's head and neck, replied, "Nope," before lighting him up.

The giant mouse did a kind of hillbilly jig right there in the middle of the street, before Clara felt the voltage wither away in her hand after less than a minute. Pulling it back and looking at the small black plastic box, she shook her head. "Why is it that this stuff always looks so good on the television, and then you buy it," and she threw it at the giant mouse, "and it ends up being a piece of shit?"

Before the giant mouse could answer, the first of the motorized scooters came over the curb and slammed into him with such force even the manufacturer would have been impressed. First Henry, then Edna, and then the twins, though the deal was sealed when the giant mouse's carpeted leg got hung up on Estelle's motorized scooter, and she dragged him a good thirty feet farther down the blacktop before finally bringing her vehicle to a stop.

Clara was standing over the stunned and broken giant mouse when Mara came up behind her. "Hey," she said, rolling around to look into her sister's eyes. "You're okay, right?"

Clara reached out and took Mara's hand. "You know, it's funny," Mara said. "You always hear about the games and parties at Chuck E Cheese," she gave the giant mouse a kick, "but you never hear anyone say whether the food's any good or not."

Lights under the pool water created a kaleidoscopic effect around the motel courtyard: shimmering reflections of aqua and silver bobbing and pulsing through the semi-darkness. It smelled like chlorine and night air. Clara, hair clipped back, barefoot in shorts and a T-shirt, leaned against the second-floor railing in front of her room and looked down at everyone on deck chairs next to the water. Even though it was after midnight, she didn't think anyone in her group would be turning in anytime soon, although so far it was just Mara, old Henry, and the Rosenthal sisters that she could see poolside, all talking and no doubt embellishing the day they'd just had. She lit a cigarette and looked over to a group of six, *early to mid-twenties maybe?* that were around a deck table somewhat farther around the pool. They were all in swimwear, wet, with a cooler, and a radio tuned to the local top forty station, cooing out tomorrow's nostalgia.

Clara was looking at, but not really registering, what they were doing, until something made her aware that all six of them had been looking up into the sky overhead, one or two of them pointing, and then resuming their conversation with each other. She too then, on reflex, looked up into the brilliant wash of stars across the sky dome overhead. Not a cloud to be seen. Just looking at it had an almost cleansing effect, and her eyes cleared as she began to turn back.

Something was up there, moving.

Holding the rail tight, she leaned out a bit farther and scanned the sky above. Was she seeing things, reflections? No. Something was definitely up there, way up there, circling slowly, almost camouflaged against the deepness. She squinted to try and make it out. She was still puzzling it over, *a kite maybe?* when she realized that a couple of the young folks in the group were looking at her, looking up.

A girl with a beach towel wrapped around her waist stepped forward and waved to Clara, calling up, "It's a hawk."

Clara looked up at it again, still unable to place it. She looked back, and registered skepticism, "A bird, at this time of night?"

"No, she's right," said the golden surfer who came up behind the beach towel and put his arm around her. "We noticed it this morning, and then again when we got back this afternoon." He looked up at it circling overhead. "It's crazy, huh? It's been up there all day."

The entire group of six, plus Clara, was again back to watching the shape moving across the upper atmosphere, when another of the young men in the group spoke out. "It's a Guardian."

Hmmm? Clara thought, as she looked over to where the boy with the long black hair was twisting a string of puka shells around his neck with his fingers. He stood still and ran both his hands across the top of his head, leaning back and staring skyward.

"It's a Guardian," he said again. "First Nations will tell you it's a protector, the hawk." He turned and looked up to where Clara was standing at the railing. Pointing up with his finger, "He's not hunting." The boy looked away and up again. "It's the Guardian." And he walked off, rejoining his group by the pool.

* * *

"You know, after a day of flying around on those motorized scooters, I don't think this old chair is going to cut it for much longer." Clara looked down the railing to where Edna Little was leaning into rolling her wheelchair over to where she was standing. Edna held her hand up as if to say, "Don't," when she saw Clara move to help her.

"Well," Edna said, coming to stop next to Clara. "That was quite the day, wasn't it?"

Clara smiled, "Yes," she said, nodding and laughing lightly. "Yes, it was." She turned to Edna, seriousness creeping in, "And Nelson, he's all right, yes?"

"Oh, he's fine all right." She dropped her head, shaking it a bit. "You know, I almost dread being back home with him." She looked up at Clara. "Do you have any idea how many times I'm going to have to hear that story?"

Just then clapping and laughing from poolside drew their attention, and they looked up in time to see Officer Nelson Little pushing Estelle in her wheelchair over to where the group had gathered. Old Henry had gotten up and was loudly, "*Bah-bah-da-bahh*-ing" as they approached, hopping over to grab Officer Little's arm with one hand and slapping him on his back with the other; the twins were side by side, beaming at him. Clara stood there and watched Officer Little soak it all in good-naturedly, still dressed in his full uniform, his hand freshly bandaged, eyes smiling like two flashlights shining out the front of his head.

"You must be very proud of your son," Clara said to Edna's back. *I have a son too*, she didn't say. Her shoulders dropped, and she deflated slightly inside. Clara opened her mouth, and it did not come out like she'd been rehearsing it. *If I've been a disappointment as a mother*, a voice in Clara's mind whispered, *and I admit it. Then what kind of mess am I if I'm transferring that disappointment onto my son, my son who I feel I don't even know?* She realized that she'd been looking up into the sky, and when she lowered her head, she saw that Edna was looking at her.

"Oh dear," Edna smiled, "you are all tangled up, aren't you?" For a moment they both just sat there and said nothing. Finally Edna looked away, staring down at the pool.

"I wanted big things when I was growing up on my father's farm, way up north," Edna was saying. "I came here and did okay. It wasn't everything I'd hoped, but it was more than I'd had, so it became enough. I had a son, and I projected all of my dreams onto him." She was looking at Officer Little through the railing. "When he became a policeman, in town, and seemed completely fulfilled, I have to admit," and she made Clara know it, "I was disappointed." She hesitated for a moment: in thinking, in talking, in breathing.

"There was a family who lived next door to us as Nelson was growing up. Their son and my boy were the same age. I never knew why, but they were never friends, barely even spoke." Edna was reaching back, now and Clara silently allowed herself to follow. She could see it all.

"Years later, after the boy had grown and married, he inherited his parents' house and moved back in with his wife and their teenage daughter. He was a foundry man, a good man by all accounts. His wife worked the register at the Five & Dime. I just knew her to wave, that was all." She paused for a moment. "And it can happen to anyone, I guess. When I saw the report on TV that there'd been an accident, a local girl had been drinking at a party, never should have been drinking; never should have tried to drive her daddy's car home ... mmh. You know how it is in a small town, our town, yes? You find out," she was looking away now. "You find out. Somehow."

"The car next door was gone, wasn't in the driveway. I stood in the front room with the lights off and could see across the yards that their only car, the only one they owned, wasn't in the driveway. He wasn't moving; he was just standing out there alone in the front yard, in the dark. Hoping." Edna reached out and grabbed Clara's hand again. "When I saw Nelson's patrol car turn in down the street, when it pulled up without lights in front of our neighbor's house, well," and her tone became strict, "I saw the mother in the front kitchen window. She was standing there in the dark watching her husband out in the yard, alone and screaming into a dish towel as my son walked across her front yard."

"So now I understand. Those folks moved out years ago now, and you know Nelson still receives handwritten letters once in a while, and I see the name on the return address." She paused again. "I never ask, and I don't want to know. What I do know is that when I see my son and how he carries himself, the way he looks at other people, his nature and sense of being, his purpose, I know that some people make fun of him, tearing him down, I know." She was holding her head back. "But they're the lesser for it. I don't know where he gets it. It sure as hell isn't from me. But whatever it took or wherever he finds it, he did find it," she pulled on Clara's arm, looking directly at her, "and they all do eventually find it. We are all disappointed in our sons, and we love them anyway. I thought that my son's life picked up where mine left off, that it was a continuation. Now I know better. We all meet in the middle, and it's the time that we are together that we carry with us as we go on alone. For me, there are no more disappointments in my life, no regrets."

*   *   *

"Damn," Mara said as she watched the pizza delivery boy step out of his car into the motel parking lot. "We were hoping you were going to blow the thirty-minutes-or-less delivery offer."

"Hey, you're lucky you're getting any at all," the delivery boy said, carrying an armful of cardboard boxes over to the revelers. "We stop taking orders at 2:00 a.m., and you just made it."

Clara and Edna watched from the upper-level railing as the two groups on the pool deck, floating through ambient lighting, finally merged into one, the cardboard boxes and the cooler suddenly, without anyone actually saying anything, open to all.

"Here you go, smart ass," Mara chided him, tossing a beer from the cooler over to the delivery boy, who caught it with one hand. "It's two oh one; you just made it."

*   *   *

"We are bright shining lights."

Clara turned and looked to Edna, who was looking down at the gathering below. "All of us," said Edna, who wasn't making much of an effort to be heard, "are like lightbulbs that click on at one end in the dark. We burn and shine our filaments all the way across, popping in the end, back into the dark."

Edna leaned forward and stuck her arm through the railing, pointing at the surf-boy. "You!" she exclaimed, drawing his attention. "What's that in your cooler?"

"Uhh, beverages, ma'am," he sheepishly replied.

"Beverages?" Edna retorted. "Son, I may look like your grand-mother ..." she let it hang out there.

The surfer's towel-clad girlfriend was laughing at him now. "They're beers, ma'am, Steel City beers." He put his hands on his waist and looked toward the ground, embarrassed.

"Right. That's fine." Edna clapped her hands together. "If you don't mind, we'll need a couple of those up here, if you please."

*   *   *

Far above a hawk continued circling, watching; watching over.

nd finally tonight we have a follow-up to a story many of you may remember from late last week. For that we'll turn it over to Marjorie Marigold. What do you have for us, Marjorie?"

"Thanks, Beth. As you can see, I'm here in the parking lot of the Convention Center, where in the midst of the Twenty-First Century Tulip Extravaganza, one of the more unusual crime sprees of recent memory has apparently come to an end."

A crowd was gathering behind where the newscaster was standing, and as the cameraman pulled back to give viewers a sense of what it was like, people began waving and mugging for the lens.

"As many viewers will remember, it was only just over a week ago that the robbery by a costumed gunman, in the southwestern part of the state during a children's birthday party, sent shock waves through the community. In that instance, not only did the gunman slip through the law enforcement dragnet that had been set up, but a member of the local police department was shot and injured while intervening to protect a small child during the commission of that crime."

Slowly but surely, the crowd behind the newscaster was growing, as more and more of the people milling around realized it was a live television feed.

"Well, tonight we're happy to report that it looks like justice has been served. As it would appear, tonight just before sunset, the Chuck E Cheese establishment here in the Gourmand Center Plaza was the scene of a heated showdown between the now-infamous Giant Mouse Bandit and the man many are calling a hero. And if you think the story ends there, Beth, you're in for a real surprise."

The crowd was now struggling from within as more and more people tried to get on camera. Astute viewers, when the newscaster was motioning toward the shopping center, caught in the background a glimpse of several people running right out into traffic in an attempt to get across the road and into the shot.

"Okay, I'm hooked, Marjorie. What's the scoop?"

"Beth, this may seem hard to imagine, and the police are not releasing any more information until a full investigation has been completed, but word is that the Giant Mouse Bandit was apprehended by the same police officer that was shot and injured in the initial robbery down state a week ago!"

"Okay, that is amazing! Tell us, how does it appear that this came about?"

It was hard to tell who started it, but once one person starting pushing and shoving, it led to bad vibes all around, and soon people in the crowd were being grabbed by their clothing and swung around, in some cases falling to the ground.

"Beth you're not going to believe this, but earlier we met up with a group of people who not only claimed to have witnessed the incident, but went on camera to say that they were actually here as part of a group that included the hero policeman! For that let's go to the tape."

* * *

"Okay, sir, and your name is?"

"I'm Henry Reinhardt, and this is Estelle Seybold, and over here are Ruby and Rosie Rosenthal."

"It's nice to meet all of you. You say that you saw the altercation earlier this evening and that you know the officer involved, is that right?"

"Sure," old Henry was saying, ignoring the newscaster altogether and staring directly into the camera lens. "Officer Nelson Little. He's our escort up here to the Tulip Festival. And can I just say," whereby old Henry got between the newscaster and the camera, "that this Tulip Festival has been fantastic and that if anyone from the nursing home is watching this, you can go ahead and sign me up for next year's trip right now."

"Well, that's wonderful, sir, and we're all glad you've enjoyed your time here, but back to Officer Nelson Little. Do you have any idea how it is that he would be here at the same time that the Giant Mouse Bandit was executing his next crime?"

"Well I can only imagine that Officer Little used our trip as cover for his continuing investigation." The entire row of motorized scooters was now nodding in unison.

"So you're saying that he was working undercover and that the apprehension this evening was the result of continuing police work on the part of Officer Nelson Little, is that right?"

"Certainly," old Henry said, as if there could be no doubt. "Officer Nelson Little is a pillar of our community and represents what is best in all of our neighbors back home."

*   *   *

The police had moved into the crowd now and were systematically moving through the throng with shields and batons. The crowd, for its part, wasn't giving up the fight, and a tussle ebbed and flowed like a wave behind where the newscast was being recorded.

"Marjorie, that is fantastic, and what a way to end the week!"

When the tape was reviewed later, it was determined that there could be no way to accurately say who exactly released the canister of tear gas, but there was no doubt that it had happened. The orange cloud erupted from the middle of the morass and soon floated over top of where the newscaster was in the middle of signing off.

"... from the parking lot outside the Convention Center here in the state capital, this is Marjorie Marigold wishing everyone a wonderful weekend."

Astute viewers saw her bend over and retch just before the shot flipped back to the studio crew.

*   *   *

The rookie held up the remote control and clicked off the television set. For several minutes afterward there wasn't a sound in the entire police station, as all that had witnessed the broadcast found themselves unable to fully process what they'd just seen.

Finally the chief came out from behind his desk and, with his fingers dug up under his glasses, rubbing his eye, he began making his way toward the door. He didn't have to say he was leaving, going home for the night.

The rookie hitched his thumbs into his belt loops and, sticking his stomach out toward the television set, proclaimed, "Jesus H. Christ!"

The chief ceased his homeward progression to turn and wearily frown at the rook. "What did you just say?"

From behind the windshield the raindrops mottled against the glass, lending a soft focus to the house, mirroring her thoughts as she looked up at the windows behind which her sister lay sleeping. In the early morning darkness, the cooler air moving over the town signaled to no one but her that something was changing. She'd known that it would happen, and the anxiety she felt curling up in her stomach told her that the time had come. The clock was ticking.

* * *

"You're thinking about leaving, aren't you?" said Mara.

She was in her pajamas, with a plaid wool coat draped on her shoulders, sitting at the kitchen table staring over a plate of dry waffles at Clara. The two of them sat there and looked at each other. It was a question that didn't require an answer.

Those were beginning to add up, Clara thought, sensing that Mara was right. She must have known it herself, before, but she only just realized it now, admitted it; seeing what she couldn't with her eyes, reflected back to her through her sister's intuition. It was when she felt that she had to that not wanting to washed over her. She closed her eyes to keep from seeing it realized, and lit a cigarette to keep from talking.

"You're not going to tell me, are you?" said Mara.

Clara wasn't cross at her, and she wasn't frustrated with the inquiries. But there was a heightened seriousness through which everything was now being filtered: an elemental concoction of familiarity, concern and trust. Something seemed wrong, and her sister was dialing into that frequency with an accuracy reserved for very few. Clara would only let Mara see that she couldn't say, and Mara would never ask more, and know anyway.

* * *

She stood in the dark bedroom and watched her sister turning in a dream. Mara was on top of the sheets, still wrapped in her plaid wool coat, waffle crumbs nestled in a warm web of static electricity. *Take a good look*, Clara thought to herself, *and make it back*. She bent down and rested her forehead on her sister's cheek for a moment before grabbing her tote bag and quietly pulling the door shut behind her.

* * *

She turned the ignition, and the engine turned over. She clicked the wiper switch, and the blades began lopping off the water. She pulled on the lights, and the road ahead presented itself. She let it all run through her mind for a minute, and the rain began rolling over the roof in sheets. She put her hand on the gearshift and pulled it down into drive. With her foot still on the brake, she saw the front door to the house open and watched as Mara ran down the walk and up to the car window.

"I love you too," Clara said out loud, stepping on the accelerator.

* * *

Facing east through the driving curtain of rain, a gray sunrise took place without anyone else noticing. Clara leaned back against the hood of the car, having pulled off under an interstate overpass to ride out the washout, and watched as a beat-up pickup truck followed suit, pulling in and behind where she was sitting. She drew deeply on her cigarette and, making note of the out-of-state tags, watched as the small, solid man with the large white cowboy hat got out of the cab, which was stuffed to the rim with cardboard boxes, and walked around to the flatbed. He whipped back the blue plastic tarpaulin and exposed several people underneath, including the son, who jumped up and stuck his chest out at his father, and the mother, wrapped in a blanket. The cowboy laughed, speaking quietly before lifting the child out and onto the roadside. The two began an inspection of their vehicle, walking its perimeter, the father speaking knowingly and pointing things out to the son—the son soaking it all in through quiet, narrowed eyes.

There's everything you have, thought Clara.

When she finally noticed that the mother was looking at her, she refocused and smiled back, immediately sensing the relief that crossed between the two of them. They were safe. No one was going to ask them, or ask of them, anything. The family folded back in on each other like a circle pulling together. Even when they were not actually touching one another, they remained connected in a way that could not be viewed physically and yet was nonetheless a constant factor.

And there's something you wouldn't know anything about, thought Clara.

Together, alone far from home, their life packed into cardboard boxes, under a piece of plastic, riding through the rain. She could have taken any one of the credit cards out of her purse and right there on the spot covered every last thing and still have come away with nothing close. The poverty of that very statement sickened her in its moral bankruptcy. Had it come to that?

Was it that emptiness inside that beckoned all manner of doubt, the psychological equivalent of use it or lose it? she thought. A self-fulfilling prophecy of that which does not live, dies?

What is it that you are not doing? she asked herself. *What's missing?*

She flicked her cigarette out into the runoff, told herself it looked like the rain had let up some, and climbed back behind the wheel.

If you're going to find it, she determined, *you're going to have to go and get it.*

Pulling back out under the leaking sky, she pressed down on the floorboard and began making up for lost time. The car swerved slightly as it picked up speed, cutting through the standing water. Clara watched as the speedometer dial stood straight up, and she held it there for a moment with her foot before the adjustment settled, and then she went further. Clicking the windshield wipers up faster, she took the steering wheel in both hands, pushed her arms out straight, locking her elbows, and dug in. The car hesitated for a moment before it lowered on its chassis and began throttling itself through the drink.

"You want it out?" she yelled to herself. *Then you're going to have to push it, force it. Outrun it. You're out here alone, and it's your life taped into a cardboard box. The clock,* she thought, *is ticking.*

As the thoughts in her head began steadying, the steering-wheel in her hands began shaking, and she bit into it with her nails and buried the accelerator. Huge plumes of water spewed up in rooster-tails behind the car as she lifted up and began to hydroplane down the interstate. The windshield wipers proved useless as the tears streamed back up and over the roof.

* * *

When the siren exploded behind her, it was like she had woken up in front of the television, and it took her a second to place where she was.

Both the car and her whole body shuddered as she pulled her foot up off the floor, and the vehicle began to sink into the roadway. She looked up into the rearview mirror and saw the blue strobe lights shimmering through the rain. Her breathing became labored, and as she hit the turn signal, she tried to retime her breath to its metronome. Pulling off onto the shoulder of the road, she pushed the transmission up into park and watched as the police cruiser pulled past and cut over in front of her.

Trembling, she took a deep breath, hugged herself, and closed her eyes.

She listened to the rain beating down onto the metal surrounding her. Finally she heard a car door slam shut, and she peered up from her chest and watched as the figure approached.

She stared straight ahead, until the tapping on the window beside her prompted acknowledgment. In the process of reaching for the window crank, her depth perception welled up an image in front of her eyes that caused her to freeze: a damaged and bandaged rain-drenched hand there on the other side of the glass. Her reengagement delayed further when movement in the door's rearview mirror drew her attention, and she had just enough time to brace herself before the transport van slid sideways and slammed into her from behind.

As far as fleshy breakdowns went, this one was right up there. *What the hell were you thinking?* Clara thought. Just then the doors opened, and Officer Nelson Little fell in behind the wheel, Mara piling into the backseat with a splash. They all sat there with the rain pounding down, looking back and forth between one another.

"So, ahh," Mara said, finally looking over at Clara, "what the hell were you thinking?"

It was while Clara was trying to come up with something to justify her behavior, something other than the truth, that she heard herself say, "I never thought it would turn out this way," surprising herself, before committing to it. She looked up at Mara. "And I feel like I'm dying inside."

She felt cold, blank, very near it.

"I got everything I wanted, everything I dreamed of." She clenched her eyes and her fists. "I'm in a world I made but can't live in."

For a moment, there wasn't anything else she needed to say.

"Now," said Mara, finally, leveling her eyes at her sister, "let me get this straight. You don't know what you want, so you up and leave everything you have behind. You spend a week with me, and then you up and leave again, the mystery girl going all speed-racer on me until …," and she turned around and looked through the rear window at what was left of the transport van being lifted up onto the wrecker. "Oh, damn," she sulked, turning back around and staring into the seat in front of her. "How am I going to explain that?"

Officer Little looked back and forth between the two sisters sitting in the backseat of his police cruiser. His mind was racing, and his own unfulfilled dreams moved into his mouth.

"PPhhh, I'm even worse," Mara concluded, continuing to sulk. "There are no silly dreams, only people who do and people who won't allow themselves to. I stayed home and wanted everything you had," and she reached out and slapped Clara on the arm, "and got nowhere close." She scrunched up her face. "If your dreams came up short, at least you tried. Mine are like wax figures in some unrealized museum, old dust-covered imitations."

Officer Nelson Little, having followed every detail of the conversation closely, opened his mouth and began, "I've always …," until a loud rapping on the driver's side window drew everyone's attention. He swallowed his dream proclamation and reluctantly rolled down the glass.

"Okay, Officer," the tow truck driver said, bending down to look in the window from under his hat as the rain poured off it to one side. "That looks like everything," and he swerved his head over to where the wrecker had chained up the transport van. "The car's drivable, so I'll follow behind it, and then you folks can get on back home."

Mara leaned up onto the back of the front seat, crossing her arms and nesting her head on them. "Thanks," she said to Officer Little. "We'll see you back home then?" she ensured, before grabbing Clara's arm and pulling her out into the rain with her.

*   *   *

When the siren exploded behind Mara, it was like she had woken up in front of the television, and it took her a second to figure out what was going on.

"What the hell?" she said, pulling off onto the berm of the road. Clara and Mara turned and watched the figure approach from behind.

Officer Nelson Little limped up through the rain and alongside the car, where he bent down and with his one good hand on a knee, took a deep breath and turned to make eye contact with the Kozlowski sisters through the glass. The three of them looked at each other for a couple of moments before Mara finally reached over and rolled the window down.

"I ..." Officer Nelson Little stuttered, looking away quickly. "Sometimes I dream of the sea."

He shrugged his shoulders and shuffled in place nervously before looking back at them. Embarrassing.

"I've never seen the ocean."

s he in there? Can you see him?" They huddled together and pressed against the motel room's window, cupping their hands and peering in through the thin gap in the curtains.

"Shhh. He's in the back, but I can't tell what he's doing."

"It's so dark in there. Why wouldn't he turn on a light?"

"Quiet, he'll hear you," whispered Clara, turning to look disapprovingly at Mara, before turning back and going right up against the glass. "I … I just, I just don't know. I can't see." She pulled back and, with her hands on her hips, frowned at the window.

"Oh, to hell with this." Mara threw her hands down at her sides. "I'm going in," and she made for the door.

"No, don't!" Clara emphasized as much as she could through her teeth, under her breath.

"Look," Mara said, holding the door knob as the smile worked its way across her face, "it's unlocked." She was giddy, laughing through her nose while trying to keep it together. Clara was looking around to see if anyone was watching them when Mara threw open the door.

"What's going on in here?" Mara yelled in her best authoritarian voice, taking two big strides into the room and pointing across it.

Startled, Officer Nelson Little shot straight up and knocked his suitcase off the edge of the bed. All his clothes spilled out onto the floor. He stood there with his mouth open looking at the two sisters silhouetted against the open door.

"Are you ...?" Mara said, going all casual and walking up to the pile of shirts and pants. "You are." She nodded, turning to look at Clara quickly before looking back. "You're folding your clothes and putting them in the motel dresser."

"Well, I ...," he waved his arms around in slight befuddlement. "It ... seemed like the right thing to do," sounding more like an excuse than he meant it to.

"Tell him," Mara said, walking back to stand next to Clara, "no one does that. You're on vacation. What you want to do is just ... wait a minute." She stepped over and looked at the clothes lying on the floor. "No, you did not."

Officer Nelson Little seemed thoroughly confused and stared down at the heap of his belongings, and then back over to Mara.

"Oh my god," she said reaching down and pulling out a shirt, holding it up for Clara to see. "You did! You packed an entire suitcase of nothing but police uniforms!" she exclaimed, wagging the crisp blue collared shirt through the air.

Clara was smiling and feeling sorry for Officer Little at the same time as she watched Mara mixing it, and him, up.

"Who does that, huh?" Mara asked, cocking her head and looking at him sternly, doing her best to maintain the illusion.

"Well, they are very utilitarian," was the best he could come up with, and it didn't even sound convincing to him as he heard his words die in the air around them.

"I know, you're not from this planet, right?" Mara tossed the shirt at him, and he stood there, letting it hit him in the chest before dropping to the floor. "This is all new to you, and you're just trying to fit in among the human race." She walked right up to him and stared hard, squinting and inquisitive.

At a complete loss, all Officer Nelson Little could do was stand there with his mouth open and his arms outstretched as if prostrating himself before some higher power.

"Well, you're in luck, mister," Mara winked at Clara before poking a finger in Officer Little's chest. "My sister here has a credit card, that for undisclosed and classified reasons, has an unlimited top end, and," she drew this out, not paying Clara's gasp any attention, " … I saw one of those twenty-four-hour Big Marts across the street when we pulled in here."

She put her arm around Clara's shoulder. "We'll be out front waiting. You get yourself together, and then we're going shopping."

Plastic lawn furniture and plastic water coolers and plastic whiffle-ball bats and plastic dolls, all lined up in rows fresh off the boat from somewhere far overseas to satisfy all your consumer needs. Clara held out her arm, her hand lightly brushing the hard, textured surfaces as she strolled past, down one aisle and up the other. They would never go anywhere, the eternal life of inanimate objects. *While you, on the other hand,* she thought, *were 100 percent biodegradable.*

You're Miss America, coming down the catwalk of life un-perturbed. And then one day you wake up, and there's a tree limb growing out the middle of your back. Show's over. The author of that beauty may or may not have been an idiot, she shook her head, but a point was to be had there somewhere.

She stopped in front of a turnstile of sunglasses. Picking one with bright red frames and dark black lenses, she slipped them on and looked around. "Hhhmmmm," she trilled and resumed her reconnaissance. She slowed and stared at the couple holding hands coming down the aisle toward her. *Now, you can't see what I'm thinking*, she thought at them as they went by, warily noting her uninterpreted inflection.

She stopped and peeked through a stack of plastic storage crates at Officer Nelson Little, who, on the other side, was frowning his way through a rack of swimming trunks.

That guy, she thought.

Reaching up and taking an aerosol can of something called Sea Breeze off the shelf, she sprayed the wet scented fluoro-carbons into the air over herself, breathing it in and letting the wood-alcohol-tinged cloud dissolve around her thoughts.

That guy, on the surface, she thought, hiding behind the stacks of plastic, *would seem to have trouble taking a pee without getting the front of his pants wet, and yet ...* She'd seen him break a line and bring them across safe at the Cow Palace. She'd seen him rush death and take the hit, and keep on ticking. She was crouching now, inspecting through the dark plastic filters his indecision between a plain blue pair and a plain red pair of swim trunks.

Where's that come from? she wondered. *Was it an effort on his part, or just an instinct?* Was it exclusive to some, like him? Or was it achievable for all. *Like me,* she put to herself. Assertiveness was the substance of the question for the moment.

She crept out from between the crates and quickly made her way up behind him, gliding to a soft-footed stop beside him. He turned, holding one pair in each hand, and opened his mouth to say ...

And was silenced as Clara reached out and plucked off a pair of blue trunks covered with red lobsters on them, and held it up under his eyes. He silently lowered his arms and took the choice from her, while she moved in, frowning at him through the bright red sunglasses with dark black lenses, and with her arms straight down at her sides, knocked against him, shoving him back slightly, before moving off and leaving him unresolved.

"Attention, shoppers!" boomed, and both Clara and Officer Nelson Little broke character to turn and watch Mara, with a huge wicker sunhat on, come rolling down the aisle on a motorized scooter, pulling up to a stop in front of them.

"Holy shit," she exclaimed. "You know we really missed out back there at that casino, not getting a couple of these for ourselves." She ran her hand down the armrest as a sign of approval. "I'll never walk in a Big Mart again."

"Really," Clara questioned. "Where'd you get that thing anyway?"

"Boy-Manager back there," Mara hooked a thumb toward the front of the store. "I told him I had plantar-fasciitis and he let me take one out." She was obviously enjoying herself. "Hey, come on, throw that stuff in and let's go. Did you know they sell cotton candy in bags?" she said, whirring off down the aisle. "It's a long trip to the end of the road!"

Clara sat in the police cruiser's backseat and pretended to sleep as they blew through the predawn darkness. Rolling through one town after another, each new one more like the tiny lighted village under a Christmas tree than the last—the looming black and green silhouetted forests next to small wooden houses, framed against a pallet of stars; open farmland, the crops frosted with a layer of mist, filling the spaces between single flashing traffic lights at empty intersections. She saw a light go on in the glass windows of a restaurant and felt it resonate in herself. Peeking over at Officer Nelson Little, steady behind the wheel, and Mara, slouched over in the passenger seat snoring away, her mind cleared.

They came and got me, she thought.

The soft rumble of the roadway passing beneath her feet mixed in her ears with the air blowing in from the slightly lowered window, a rich grassy scent lightly tickling her nose. She sat wrapped in a woolen blanket, warm and dry, feeling clean and safe for the first time in what seemed like a long time. Nestling into the corner between the seat and the door, she relaxed and eased back. Through the opposite window she watched the blinking lights of an airplane, high above and far away, cutting parallel with her across the dark canvas above. *All those people*, she thought, *going where?* On some great adventure in their lives, this one time together for a ride through the night sky, a mysterious faraway city to be explored? Were they surrounded by loved ones, people who cared for them? Or were they waiting at the end of the road, anticipating their arrival? She shivered excitedly at the slim chance, the happy small thought, of someone on the plane looking down and watching the tiny lights of the police cruiser speeding across the rich black landscape far below, and wondering who she was, where she was going, and if she was surrounded by people who loved her. It felt somehow magical, and she stared harder at the little jet flashing across the universe. *Take a picture of this and remember how you feel*, she thought. She snuggled deeper into the corner, holding herself, and stole a glance at the rearview mirror and the eyes reflected therein, and listened to the rhythmic labored breathing within arm's reach.

They haven't left me behind, she silently mouthed to herself.

The plan had been to rise early and push for the shore, drive all day, and get in with the sunset. At the time, she hadn't thought it wise; it seemed like an unnecessary rush, but hadn't said anything. She hadn't slept, lying there on the motel bed next to her sister. Unable to stop thinking in the unfamiliar darkness about unfamiliar considerations, her mind had raced, playing out all manner of possibilities concerning what she was doing and, possibly more important, what she wasn't.

She no longer knew how she felt, and that, in and of itself, seemed a relief. It had taken until now for her to find a level place to stand and consider her options. She may not have gotten any closer to a decision, but with that solidity she at least now felt she was in a position to make one. Cast off all but what you knew to be true: there was the possibility that she was ill and that for her own peace of mind she had to deal with it any way she could. Do what she alone felt was right, and maybe, just maybe, she would come out the other side whole in spirit.

That was all that mattered.

Everything else was bullshit.

And now, wrapped in her prickly cocoon, in the police car being driven on through the increasingly pinkish-blue air toward the seaside, she anticipated the awaiting expanse. With the prospect of a therapy of elements, ocean and sky, cooling her mind, she whispered, *good-bye* as her little jetliner disappeared into a cloud, and sleep washed over her.

There was no longer a need to pretend.

*   *   *

"Go ahead and hit 'em with that siren one time," Mara said, pointing to the police cruiser's dashboard and looking at the car tooling along at the speed limit in front of them. "That'll wake their butts up."

Officer Little carefully signaled and then moved into the passing lane. Clara was roused by her sister's voice and the sudden shift in the car's progression. She sat up just enough to see into the vehicle they were passing.

"Oh boy," Mara grimly pronounced as they went by, "will you look at that."

Behind windows rolled up tight against the rest of the world, behind the firmly gripped steering wheel, a man was yelling in synchronicity with the woman yelling next to him, a screaming baby in her lap. Hardly constrained by seat belts, more yelling (though some of this was visually indistinguishable from laughter) via strands of intertwined teenage DNA in the backseat. All of which to the casual observer both set them apart from themselves and identified them with every family working through spending so much quality time together after fifty-one weeks apart.

"You know, if we were flying that's probably who would get seated right behind us," Mara observed, turning back around and noticing that Clara was now awake. "Well, good morning, or rather afternoon."

Still groggy, Clara closed her eyes again and asked, "What time is it?" while fishing around to light a cigarette.

Mara opened the thermos and poured out a lid-top full of coffee, handing it back over the seat. "It's almost two o'clock; you've been out like a light all morning."

Clara took the coffee and breathed it in, mixing it with the smoke and giving in to the cumulative stimulation. "Mara," she spoke, "can I ask you a question?"

Officer Nelson Little immediately sensed that maybe he shouldn't be here and pulled himself out of the rearview mirror, refocusing on the road ahead. Mara leaned onto the seat and looked at her sister, "Sure, anything."

"Well," she began, trying to formulate her still-waking thoughts. "Remember when you said that my dreams were also your dreams?" She looked up at Mara. "Was that true? Was that all you thought about, really?"

Caught off her game, Mara came up puzzled for a moment as she tried to figure out what Clara was getting at. "Yeah, I mean, I guess, you know," she rocked her head back and forth as if shaking out the thoughts. "Sure I wanted all that, what can I say?" she shrugged, "maybe I was a little jealous of you too."

Clara seemed pained in her expression as she listened. "Really," she said, "that's all? There was nothing else?"

Mara frowned and lowered her tone, glancing over to Officer Little before quickly turning back. "Well, of course not. Or, I mean, yeah, I wanted that and more, sure. You want a list? That's what you're asking?" Clara's nonresponse spoke volumes, and Mara continued.

"Okay, well," she was thinking out loud now, "I always wanted to see an opera, you know? And not one of those dinky regional things but the real deal, a big cosmopolitan blowout. The more outlandishly over-the-top the better, ha!" she laughed. "Lawman here wants to see the ocean. Yeah, I want to fly over it one day, stand on the other side and long to be home."

She opened her eyes, and the smile vanished, staring at Clara imparting seriousness. "And there's some reading I will do: *Innocents Abroad* and *Tales from Beyond the Global Village*, something each by Leslie Marmon Silko and William Gaddis. I will make the time for these." Clara watched Mara seal these private envelopes, making mental notes not to forget, reiterating past desires.

"You know what's funny, though?" she asked Clara. "Right now I wouldn't change anything, here with you," she turned and shoved Officer Nelson Little, "and you too." She looked happy when she told Clara, "I'm happy; I'm enjoying this."

Clara flicked her cigarette butt out the police car's window and cleared a space in her mind for a new list. *It starts now*, she thought.

"Here," Mara uncrumpled the paper bag between her and Officer Little, pulling out a tin-foil-wrapped handful. "Breakfast. It's kind of like an egg on muffin," she said handing it over the seat to Clara, "only with no egg and no muffin." Clara took the hot dog and unwrapped it; she was hungry and wasted no time in having at it.

"Wow," Mara watched as Clara tore into her breakfast. "You gotta love hot dogs. They taste good, and they remind you that sometimes you just have to *live* your life."

Clara froze in midchew. "What was that?"

"Oh, I don't know," Mara said, "something the old man who sold them to us said. You were out of it back there when we pulled in to the rest area, and this crazy old guy was grilling hot dogs in the parking lot."

"What!" Clara exclaimed, sitting forward and swallowing.

"What do you mean, 'What'," said Mara. "Good Samaritan here was the one who actually talked to him." She looked over at Officer Little. "Hell, look at this." She held up the brown bag, "He bought everything the old guy had. Christ, we could start our own scout troop with this many hot dogs."

"Was there a lady with him?" Clara inquired. "Was there a table of handcrafts?"

"I don't know; a lot of people were there," Mara was wondering in Clara's direction. "The lot was full, you know, coming and going."

Clara looked at Officer Nelson Little, who seemed to be quietly reviewing the tape in his mind, a frown on his brow signifying that he was thinking, before turning on her knees and looking out the back window. She let her thoughts drift back along with the receding highway.

"There was one thing."

Clara turned quickly back and came up behind Officer Little, putting her hands on top of the seat. "Yes, Nelson, something?" she asked.

"Well," the policeman intoned, his face twisting as if wringing the memory out. "I didn't think anything of it at the time. In fact," he looked at Clara in the rearview mirror, "I wasn't even sure he was talking to me."

Clara was looking right into his reflection, nodding with his every word.

"I was walking back to the car and I heard," he seemed almost doubtful now, "at least I think I heard, him say, 'You be careful with her out there on the road,' or, at least," he twisted again, "something to that effect."

Clara exhaled loudly and dropped back onto the seat, and then sat up and began rummaging through her purse. Grabbing out the hair barrette, she smiled at the brown hawk against the white sky before clutching it tightly in front of her and pressing it against her face. She closed her eyes, pulled her hair back, and clipped it up.

Back once again, she opened her eyes and saw across at Mara, who was clutching the brown bag and staring at her, mouth partially open and eyes registering nothing but questions.

"Hey, you don't get the whole bag," Clara said, her eyes watering. "Toss another one of those hot dogs back here. I'm starving."

Southern rock, blasting out in a northern climate, in the Western world, on the Eastern Seaboard: it's Friday evening in the United States of America. Clara Kozlowski stood eating a snow cone and looking across the boardwalk at Officer Nelson Little vomiting into a trash can next to the Tilt-A-Whirl.

"That's it; get it out," Mara said. "Now you're ready for the big one."

She put a hand on Officer Little's back as he creaked up into a standing position. "Look at that thing over there." She was pointing him down the boardwalk a bit. "It's called the Scrambler. Holy shit, that looks wild, huh? Let's see if we can get right up in the front!"

Clara smiled and shook her head before turning and walking over to the wooden railing. The sun was going down now and the whole boardwalk-midway was being enveloped in a glimmering electric halo, punctuated by the clanking metal rides, the vibrato of the music's speakers, and laughter. Standing there under the string of carnival lights, looking out toward the darkening sea, she listened to it churning and crashing onto the shore and watched the bouncing clouds of lightning ricochet across the distant horizon. The storm had raced them to the beach, beat them to it, and had already moved out to sea. The air smelled clean and fresh, salty brine on her lips and tongue when she breathed through her mouth.

She held her snow cone up, tightened her toes around the flip-flop thongs and stepped up onto the railing, balancing herself with one arm. Holding still, and holding her breath, she lifted one leg, put it over the top rail and brought it down onto the same rail on the other side. Then, quickly, she swung her other leg up and over and almost ... before she lost her balance and fell backward down onto her butt in the sand. Her flavored ball of ice popped up and out of the paper cone and plunked down next to her in the grit.

"Shoot," she remarked to herself, standing and brushing off her shorts.

Crumpling the syrupy paper funnel up, she shoved it into a pocket and pulled out and lit a cigarette. Holding her flip-flops in the other hand, she began mashing her way through the sand down to where the surf was pounding the beach.

The water was cold, even this late in the summer, and felt good washing against her legs. With each pull of the tide back, her feet sank farther into the sand beneath, and she could feel wisps of seaweed whirling around. The horizon was dotted with the lights of cargo ships making their way through the transit channels far offshore, and she watched their slow progress and relaxed, peacefully smoking and breathing.

And thinking, *There's no farther to go. It'll happen here.*

With the ocean gurgling around her, and her peripheral vision filled with it stretching out into the approaching darkness on both her left and right, she turned around and looked back across the beach toward the boardwalk. It's a long trip to the end of the road. *Damn right*, she thought. *And the road ends here.*

Standing in the surf, standing on the edge of her world, with her back to the ocean, she determined to face everything that was coming at her, and in making a small stand sensed that while she'd been looking for everything she thought her life was missing, something like it had been cradling her through the journey the whole time. *All those people*, she remembered, *who made me a part of their moments.* The ones you share and don't get back. Having searched for a reflective place to sit on the outside and look in, she suddenly wanted back in.

The wave surged into her high from behind; her feet sank, and she toppled forward and went into the surf face-down. Splashing with her arms out, she rolled over and lay on her back as the tide withdrew around her, drawing out the cigarette pack and the paper snow cone funnel from her pocket.

"Oh!" she exclaimed, snatching the cigarette-pack raft as it was just beginning its journey out to sea. She watched the paper ice cone float out of reach and then shoot past the break and across the top of the water. Sitting there in the shallow surf, she pointed at the paper cone. *I'll stay here and get it worked out.* She was overcome, happy in thinking, *and that part of me will continue on. Forever.*

She stood up, raked her wet hair back across her head with her fingers and then, laughing, ran through the sand toward the boardwalk.

* * *

167

Unsteady, flecked and greenish, Officer Nelson Little looked over at Mara Kozlowski, who, with melted red, white, and blue snow cone syrup staining both hands and the front of her shirt, looked at Clara, soaked from head to toe in flip-flops, shorts, and a T-shirt.

"Okay, change of plans," Mara said, still wiping her hands on her shirt. "It's a do-over. We'll go back to the motel and clean up, and *then* we'll go out to dinner."

No one said anything; no one had to. As they stood there together breathing at one another, eyes glowing, even if they had considered it, they wouldn't have wanted to be anywhere else.

Blue crab cakes on paper plates accompanied by coleslaw liberally sprinkled with ground black pepper, eaten with a plastic spork and washed down with watered-down two dollar pitchers of beer. It wasn't the best meal she had eaten, just that in the moment she couldn't think of anything that had been any better. Sitting on the bench seat of a wooden picnic table at Fat Chance's Tiki Hut boardwalk patio, Clara anchored her pile of napkins to the vinyl tablecloth with a sweating plastic mug and leaned onto her elbows. She closed her eyes and let the rest of her senses take over.

The breeze from the ocean found its way through her hair, and she could feel it coursing across her scalp and down the back of her neck. Her nose was filled with the scent of coconut suntan lotion, malt vinegar, saltwater taffy, and the occasional punctuations of alcohol, tobacco, and the sea. The intermingling of music from different sources and the overwhelming overlapping of the voices from conversations moving by, hovering around and the one she belonged to, created a symphony of alliterative pitches and intonations that only the side effects of cheap beer could delineate. She felt for her cigarette pack, felt that it was empty, and took a long draw on her beer while looking around for the bar.

"Oh yessssssssss!" Mara exclaimed, standing. "Listen. It's that new wave beach song thing, ha! Hey," she leaned down onto her palms in front of Clara, "dance with me, huh?"

Clara smiled at her and pendulum-swung her empty pack back and forth in tandem with her shaking head. "Sorry, but I've got some shopping to do," she said flipping the pack up onto the tabletop. Mara turned and, without saying a word, extended her hand in the direction of Officer Nelson Little. As had become her new guilty pleasure, Clara couldn't resist smiling into his now hesitant eyes.

A look on his face suggested that he'd been rehearsing for just this scenario. "But I don't think I'd … better. I've never," Officer Little squeaked out, before clearing his throat, "danced before."

"Come on," Mara snapped her fingers at him. "You see, this is all part of the realization of your dream." She was laughing and overtly making it up as she went along. "The part you're just now remembering. You wouldn't let a gunshot wound and a couple of dog bites hold you back from fulfilling the promise now, hmm? After coming all this way? Come on," she ordered, "let's go!"

And with that she scooped the policeman up in her personality and led him out onto the floor. Clara sat and watched her sister bopping under the swirling lights, pogoing around and around the contender for World's Most Awkward Individual. She had to admit it looked like fun. *If they're still at it when you get back,* she thought, on standing and heading over to the bar, *then you're cutting in.*

*   *   *

Like any bartender worth his or her margarita's salt, he saw her coming and met her halfway. Tossing the towel over his shoulder, he placed both hands on the counter and leaned a shaved scalp into the question.

"More of these?" Clara presented her empty pack as exhibit number one.

"Sure thing," he called out and turned to running a finger down the rack of packs on the mirrored back wall.

Clara fished out a handful of bills from a pocket and on laying them out in front of her, turned and, for a moment, looking into the eyes looking at her, was struck with a mix of something bordering on confusion, awe, and fear. She pulled back and blinked repeatedly, almost drawing away completely, until she realized that the bird, the very big bird, actually, was watching from behind bars. *My god*, she mouthed. She'd never seen anything like it, up so close, before.

"That's Polly," the bartender said on returning and presenting the cigarette pack. "And before you say it, yeah, I know, a tiki hut should have a parrot, and that ain't no parrot."

The hawk stood erect and balanced on a wooden pole, tethered to the cage from a leather band around one clawed leg, and observed Clara with an unyielding continuity. A calm gracefulness seemed to emanate from the bird, and to Clara it seemed to suggest an air of patience, as if it was simply waiting for something that it knew would happen eventually.

Clara watched the hawk watch the bartender make change and then shift its gaze back to her. Without looking away, she asked, "How on earth did a hawk end up in here anyway?"

"Ah, well," the bartender started. "You know one thing about Fat Chance is he's a stingy old SOB, and parrots, as you can imagine, cost hard cash. So," and he turned to look at the hawk, "when he bean-bagged old Polly here off the telephone pole out in front of his house, well, that's money in the bank to his way of thinking. And you know," he turned to survey the clientele, "most of these folks wouldn't know a parrot if it flew down and pooped in their eye. Hell," he swung his arm around toward the bird, and Clara watched it take note of the attention, "I stood here once and watched this drunken guy spend the better part of a night trying to get her to ask for a cracker." His lopsided attempt at a smile was rounded out by the curvature of his domed head.

"Does she ever get out?"

"Polly? No," the bartender confirmed. "Us two, we're birds of a feather. Neither of us is going anywhere, ain't that right, Polly?"

Clara listened while the bartender talked, never looking away from the bird. There was something about the way it would turn and seem to listen to what was going on, and then look back at her as if to confirm she had been paying attention.

"Thank you," she said, pulling her change and the fresh pack of cigarettes toward her. Without thinking, she took the empty pack and, flipping her wrist, quickly spun it through the air, over and directly into the trash pail against the mirrored wall.

"Anytime," the bartender replied, both he and the hawk watching her walk off.

*   *   *

"Ahh, there you are," Clara said, on hands and knees, spotting her flip-flop, which had gone flying under a table quite a ways back from the dance floor. On retrieving it, she dropped its partner and stepped into them, wiggling around until settled. It was after midnight now, and that made for about as full a day as she'd had in some time. By the looks of her dance partners, she wasn't the only one who'd be sleeping in tomorrow morning either. Under the faux-thatched roof, she watched as Mara and Nelson squared the tab and gathered their things. Even from this distance, she could see the policeman breathing heavily as he recovered from his whirlwind indoctrination into the perils of modern dance. Her sister, on the other hand, probably could have gone another couple of rounds, though by the end even she was having a time keeping herself on an even keel. As for Clara, she took the projectile flip-flop as a sign that some part of her was ready to call it a night.

Lighting a cigarette, she sat at the nearest empty table and relaxed, already ready and waiting, in no hurry. She was looking over to the bar, to the tethered and caged bird, the hawk, thinking that from this distance it looked as if it was looking back at her, when she saw something hit and bounce off the cage. Scanning the now-sparse crowd, her eyes landed on a table full of empty two-dollar pitchers ringed by the associated inebriants. She watched their buffoonery from afar; saw the shirtless trust fund with the predictable tattoos ringing his biceps hold a peanut onto the table with an index finger and then paper-football-style, flick it over and against the cage. Whooping high-fives were exchanged as another peanut was brought into position.

I didn't need to see that, crossed her mind on standing to leave.

Making her way over to where Mara and Nelson were waiting on her now, she took one more look back, and damn if that bird didn't look like it was watching her walk across the Tiki Hut, she thought to herself, never even flinching when another peanut hit the bars.

"Let's walk back in the sand," Clara suggested, and the three of them swung around and down onto the beach in front of the Tiki Hut, she and Mara each kicking off and snatching up their flip-flops as they made their way by. Clara slowed and let the other two drift a little ahead of her.

Probably right about ..., she silently judged, *there.*

Holding up her hand and flicking the cigarette butt over and into the Tiki Hut, the ensuing overheard chorus of, "Dude, what the fuck!" brought a smile to her face as she jogged to catch up.

The iridescent turquoise numerals glowed in the darkness: two o'clock in the morning. She lay sideways taking note, until eventually rolling over onto her back and putting both of her hands behind her head. How do you process your biggest self-imposed knot into something that makes sense and that you can live with? Is it possible, after you've sent one seemingly random personal idiosyncrasy after another crashing into a wall of self-doubt and uncertainty, to untangle the wreckage and string it all out into a linear thread that can be learned from and followed?

If you asked for help, would someone actually intercede between you and your indecisions? And if they could make a difference, would it make a difference to them to know that in moments of weakness you are capable of harboring doubts about the value of the effort? Are there really no guarantees in a life? Is it that you've boxed everything up, compartmentalized each aspect until there's no logical progression? Are you all in, truly committed to letting it ride; taking the chances?

Is life an all-caps verb?

She sat up on the bed. You've been observing and gathering. The necessary tools are at your disposal. When the dealer turns over that last card, it won't matter what turns up, only whether you were present and accountable when it took place.

Slightly bouncing in place, standing now in the center of the bed, with thoughts racing past one another. From wide-open eyes sweeping across the pitch-black screen of air and space, a flickering of previews hinting at an internal manifestation of possibilities. Arms reaching out unseen, grasping in earnestness. Nothing moves past the end of the road? You are not alone and were not left behind. Fear will hold you back, and assertiveness will bolster you stepping into the tidal surge of everything you fear—as you alone attempt movement beyond the end of the road.

You want it out? You're going to have to force it, she thought. *You're going to have to*, "Let it out!" she yelled, throwing her arms down at her sides in the process.

The light between the two twin beds clicked on.

Clara, sweating in the motel room's air-conditioning, stood in her T-shirt and underpants in the middle of the mattress and looked down to where Mara, under cover, was shielding her one partially open eye with a hand and looking up at her. The two of them held place and processed the moment, looking directly into each other's eyes for several minutes, before finally Mara asked, "Now? This is it, now?"

"I think so."

"Okay."

"You're ...?" Clara was shivering, her teeth chattering as she spoke.

"Of course," Mara replied, throwing back the covers and swinging around to sit on the edge of the bed, glancing over at the clock. "Wow." She took a deep breath and held her head in her lap for a moment.

"I'm a little scared."

"That," Mara sat up with her eyes closed, "is not comforting." She reached out and clicked the lamp back off. "Why don't you climb down here, and tell me what you have in mind?"

*   *   *

"Oh, man." Mara, with her hand on the door knob, looked back at Clara, who had pushed up against her. "This guy's something else," and she turned the knob and the unlocked door opened quietly. They came in on bare feet, padding silently between the two beds to stand over Officer Nelson Little, snug as a bug in a rug and snoring through his partially open mouth.

They sat down next to each other on the edge of the bed opposite, facing him. Mara had opted for a pair of black capris and a gray tank top, insisting on swathing her eyes with a dark shadow, squinting through a grin at herself in the mirror during the application ("like a Ninja!"); Clara scissored off the legs to a pair of blue jeans, pulled on a crisp forest green T-shirt and had pulled her hair back, clipping it up with the barrette.

Mara reached over and clicked on the lamp.

At first, in the slightly orange-hued incandescence, the two sisters sat and basked in the endless fascination of watching Officer Little drifting through the sluice of sleep. Inevitability, though, in spotting the direct-light-induced vibration of a tiny vein on the outside of one eyelid, they sat back and prepared for the resumption.

He closed his mouth, and a low "mmmmmhhhhphh" pushed up from his chest and against the back of his lips. At the top of a long, slow, nasal inhale, his eyes folded open and began dilating, until he achieved focus and stared sideways at the visitors sitting across from where he lay. Instant recognition prompted a calmness where the eyelids drooped and an involuntary smile spread across his face.

And then the asteroid of awareness blew through the clouds, and he sat bolt-upright. Clenching his teeth, he drew a short breath, noted the time, and opened his mouth as if to speak.

Clara wrapped an arm around Mara, who leaned forward and placed her hands flat on the sheets around where Officer Nelson Little sat.

"You," she whispered mysteriously, intimating as much in turn with her eyes through the cosmetic camouflage, "are going to need to dig out one of those uniforms."

* * *

The ship rocked in the jostling ocean waves, anchored against drift out of the transit channel. Hundreds of aluminum storage containers, moored to the open deck, creaked and groaned mournfully against the lashings, adding a reverberating soundtrack to the electrical display cracking across the sky from all around. The lone deck watchman held the rail with both hands and peered across the water at the tiny faraway boardwalk, a Ferris wheel twirling and beckoning—the most seductive of lighthouses.

Clear there now and clear here soon, he had hoped, looking up into the roiling black storm clouds overhead. "Hmm?" he frowned.

Something else was up there, moving.

*Thwaaa*aaaacccccck pierced the night, and he turned back just in time to see the mooring cable snapping and slapping across the face of the water alongside. The ship began dropping between the swells and then, on the rise and off balance, tipped slightly, held for a moment, and gave it up.

"Oh shit," the watchman grimaced.

Dulled scraping like fingernails on a chalkboard signified movement as the enormous block of stacked silver storage containers, emblazoned in an unknown calligraphy, shifted, hesitated just long enough for one to think possibly, *maybe*, and then wall by wall began toppling into the sloshing depths: a million nonrecyclable plastic knickknacks offered up for a yet-to-be-fully-determined penance in exchange for a useless immortality.

Its horn blasting now, long and low, the ship spun slightly on its chain—then, bobbing back and forth, righted itself and took a front row seat as the flotsam and jetsam of its inglorious mission floated off to a wider awareness.

★　★　★

Circling and circling and circling.

On wings from out beyond the end of the road, against a charged sky under which anything can happen, over a reflective pool of immense perception and depth, it comes to this, and the waiting ends.

Complete the circle, and head in.

Go to her.

Sooner or later you have to trust someone. Sooner or later you *want* to trust someone. He'd been very patient, and time had rewarded him with a sense of relief that felt palatable. On the best day of his life, Officer Nelson Little, in full uniform, stood under his hat and determined right there on the spot that he would not now or anytime in the future ever openly question the Kozlowski sisters. Sometimes you just knew, and it was golden.

To serve and protect.

The dogma fell away easily, and for the first time the mantra that he had always striven to aspire to came as naturally as when he'd answered, "Yes," without even having to think about it.

They needed help. They came to him. That would be enough.

He'd seen into the eyes of lies enough to know the difference, and that cynicism was a mold that clung and tainted everything that followed. He'd been a cop looking into a world that he was always just one degree removed from. You draw a line, you stay on your side, and things don't get messy.

And then these two sisters upended the whole kit and caboodle.

What a fantastic mess. There had been moments over the last several days where he'd caught himself not breathing—so caught up in the accumulation of emotions that his mind had actually felt as if it had filled and that time was needed to make room for whatever came next. Jubilation was not a word that he could have equated with his own existence prior. Now it became apparent that no matter what lay ahead, he had experienced something that, previously unable to face the sneaking possibility that nothing was there for him; he had long hid from: the *life* within his life.

There'd be no taking it back.

He would now carry it with him forever as treasure. Twenty-four hours a day today, or twenty-four years starting with tomorrow, it wasn't going to matter when—he would drop everything and pick it up right from this moment, on a moment's notice, unfettered. He would have hopes, and he would dream, and he would never openly speak of it—shielding everyone, and his determination, as one would handle a delicate gift out of fear that it might shatter under undue scrutiny. The secret to never divulge. Better to commit, hold it glowing in your mind's heart, and should the day come where they again turn your way, be prepared to remember and understand who these people were and what they had done for you.

And on his last day, he will think of all those people who had called him a friend, these sisters who looked at him differently, and that would be more than he ever thought possible.

That could be enough.

*   *   *

Pulling the visor down a little farther on his brow, Officer Nelson Little filled his lungs, crossed his arms, stood up straight, and prepared to make good on his promise that no one was going to get between him and them, and if something, anything, were to happen he would get them out safely. Looking into Mara's eyes, he'd seen a question, and in Clara's the answer. A wrong needed to be made right.

That would be enough.

Standing with his back to the shuttered front entrance of Fat Chance's Tiki Hut, he watched as the stragglers made their way by, most not even acknowledging that a policeman was present, corralling and joking with one another in small zigzagging groups. He was thinking it funny that only a short while ago he'd been sound asleep, completely unaware that all of this was still going on, when he noticed the bicycle headlamps weaving their way down the boardwalk.

The two security guards pulled up and braked in front of him, and two things came to mind right off: anyone wearing tinted eye protection at this time of night is going to display some attitude, and not everyone is flattered by tucking their shirt in.

Simultaneously lowering their kickstands, the two guards did their best synchronized dismount of the bicycles, only breaking rank while the one wobbled around freeing up his regulation shorts with one hand, and the other used both to square up his riding helmet, giving himself a little vanity check in the clip-on handlebar mirror. Confidence restored, they approached Officer Little.

"Officer," they both nodded. "Everything's good, we trust?" each one briefly tipping his head to peer around behind where he was standing.

"Yes, sirs," Officer Little answered, feet firmly planted in place.

"All right, good," nodding, acting the part. "You're ahhh ...," jutting a chin out at the uniform, "on duty?"

"No."

"Ahhhh," the one guard sensed a break in the case. "You're on vacation, then?"

"Well," Officer Little extended what was left of his left hand, "kind of."

"Oooh," both guards took note. "In the line of duty?" the one asked, lifting his eye protection and leaning in to get what seemed to be a quick sniff of the bandages before Officer Little could pull back.

Muted clattering from behind the policeman froze the moment and the policeman. Both security guards went for their batons, assuming an obviously much-practiced security stance.

"Hey," the one guard said, narrowing his tinted and protected eyes, pointing toward the Tiki Hut. "Is there someone in there?"

Folding his arms again across his chest, Officer Nelson Little never took his eyes off the crouching guards as he shook his head, "No. This establishment is closed for the night."

"Are you sure?" both guards caught themselves saying at the same time, before slowly looking over at one another as if that was a clue to what was going on.

Officer Nelson Little was in the process of formulating his next move when out of the corner of his eye he caught a fleeting trace of near-illusionary shadow, before the screech audibly atomized through the space around them, followed by the beating of air and a tremulous sense of movement from above.

"What the ...!" fumbling out flashlights and crisscrossing the sky above, both guards spent the next couple of minutes scanning the nearby roofs for intruders before determining it was a likely gull encounter. "Not too uncommon an occurrence here at the shore," the one guard assured Officer Little while reholstering his flashlight.

The action had reinvigorated the moment. With a renewed sense of purpose, they were preparing to enjoy a head back, chest out moment of professional camaraderie with a fellow law enforcement official, when the security guards suddenly realized that far offshore a long, low horn had been rhythmically blowing, its pitch and tone coming in on the surf. The entire boardwalk populace had stopped in their tracks around them, looking out toward the tiny, piercing lights dotting the horizon between sea and sky.

"Jesus, Mary, and Joseph!" the one security guard looked to the other. "That's a maritime distress call. Something's happened out in the shipping channel."

Without delay, which would have included saying good-bye, both guards hopped on their bicycles and took off pedaling at an accelerated pace down the boardwalk. Officer Little watched them go, noting the one guard stop just long enough to reach around and pull his regulation shorts out again before rejoining the pursuit.

Feet still firmly planted, Officer Nelson Little murmured small relief under his breath, checked the empty space over and around the Tiki Hut, and then settled in for as long as it would take.

He didn't even realize that he was smiling.

You do realize that next year when we take a vacation, this is going to be hard to top, right?"

"We're going on vacation together next year?"

"If there's another question here, it's why wouldn't we?"

And with her propensity for coming through supposedly locked doors apparently undiminished, Mara put her hand on the back door knob of Fat Chance's Tiki Hut, turned it, heard the lock click, and with a wry smile on her lips, pushed it open into the darkness within.

"Am I missing something here?" Clara whispered, watching yet another deterrent across her path swing open uncontested.

"Don't stop to think what we're doing," sang Mara. "I'll surprise you every time."

They stepped through the frame and very quietly closed the door behind them. Taking a minute to let their eyes adjust, they stood still and listened. The freewheeling ambient atmosphere of earlier had given way to a still life of shadowed potted palms and pink plastic flamingos. With the front shuttered against the night and the overhead fans powerless, the air inside had turned and stagnated; the scent of unmopped spills waiting for the next chance to drift away. The only thing more unforgiving than bad lighting was the memories.

"Phew. Kind of reminds you of when Dorothy pulls back the curtain in Oz, huh?"

"Come on, let's go."

"Hey, wait a minute." Mara tapped Clara's attention and, pulling her arms up against her sides, bent down at the knees and began moving across the floor in an exaggerated version of a tiptoeing cat burglar. "Walk like this."

"Psssshtt!" Clara stifled her laugh with a fist, and blew through her nose, wetting her wrist in the process. "Shit," she laughed, backing into a pile of serving trays, which then cascaded off the tabletop and down onto the floor.

"Ooo, careful," Mara mockingly reprimanded her, ceasing her prancing long enough to reach out and point at her across the dark room. "And when did you start laughing like that?"

"Yeah, thanks a lot," Clara said. "I'll note both as being your fault." She pulled a napkin out of a table dispenser and wiped her hand before bending down to start gathering the trays up.

"Ssshh!" Mara was at the front entrance now, peeking through the slats out onto the boardwalk. "Come here; look."

Standing unobserved, enveloped in the night, they looked out at Officer Nelson Little, his back to them. He was obstructing their view enough that they couldn't see exactly who he was talking to but that he was talking to anyone was cause for concern. They were both holding their breaths and watching intently through sharpened eyes when something landed on the roof right over where they were standing, its caw piercing their subconscious. In the dark, your imagination explodes.

Clara turned wide-eyed toward Mara just in time to quickly reach out and cover her opening mouth with a hand, smothering the words she didn't need to hear: *What the hell was that?* They crouched there facing one another, each with a hand out on some part of the other, until the sweeping beams of light crisscrossing the Tiki Hut drew their eyes back through the slats.

"Rent-a-cops," whispered Mara, never peeling her eyes away from the hidden vantage point out into the lights.

They watched as the two security guards moved around in front of Officer Little, ducking and weaving, waving their flashlights back and forth, up and down, searching. Mara's head went left, and then right, as she toggled between the two security guards, watching their every move. Clara became obsessed with the policeman, though. How he stood there, legs slightly splayed apart, arms crossed, unmoving, and somehow drew an imaginary line that despite there being two of them to his one, wasn't being crossed. She could see what was going on, even if she didn't know what was going on, and through it all, her perspective was from around the policeman, who remained omnipresent. It may have been her mind overreaching, playing tricks on her in the dark, an optical illusion. But whatever it was, it was beautiful, comforting, and at a time when she was floundering in self-doubt, the most visually reassuring display of self-confidence she could have hoped for. If she'd needed some kind of boost, an acknowledgment that she was doing the right thing, then that would be enough. She sat back not needing to see any more—it was going to be all right.

"Wow, look at that," Mara turned to look at Clara. "They're taking off," turning back to peek through the slats. "Hauling ass, actually. Bye-bye." She waved slightly watching them disappear from her line of sight.

*　*　*

Polly stood as before. In fact, thought Clara, she didn't appear to have moved so much as an inch. "Have you been waiting for me?" asked Clara.

"Are you talking to the bird?" asked Mara from behind her.

Clara turned to look at Mara, who had hopped up on a stool alongside and had a hand in the bowl of peanuts and pretzels left out on the bar.

"What are you doing?" Clara smirked at her sister.

"What do you mean, 'What am I doing?'" she replied. "They're out free for the customers, right?"

"Is that what we are?"

"Well," Mara declared, "we damn sure were." Popping in a mouthful, she proceeded to chew with her mouth open, all the while smiling at Clara.

Clara snorted again and turned back to the cage, placing both hands on it and running them slowly down the bronze bars. They were illuminated in moonlight leaking in through gaps in the front shutters, and the hawk was following her every move with its eyes, never moving more than to twist its head slightly in the process. "How are we going to get you out of there, hmm?" Clara wondered.

"That's a mean-looking beak," declared Mara. "Not to mention your bird is the size of a bowling pin. How about you just throw open the little gate, and then we'll make a run for it."

Clara and the hawk both turned and seemed to frown at the suggestion, before Mara shrugged an apology and stuffed in another pretzel.

"No," Clara turned back to Polly's perch. "She's tied up. It's going to take a little ...," and with that she popped open the gate on the cage and reached in past the hawk.

"Holy shit," Mara jumped off the stool and came up from behind, putting both hands flat on Clara's back. "Be careful."

Clara concentrated fully. With one hand resting on the outside of the cage, she watched as her fingers slowly worked the leather tether free, nimbly twisting and pulling as if at a shoelace knot, until it worked loose and fell apart, dropping away from the bars.

"Almost," she whispered to herself.

With her one arm still stretched across the interior of the cage, she moved it back toward the hawk, who was watching her every move in small, rapid, yellow blinking bursts of sight.

"It's okay," Clara assured. "Go ahead."

For a moment they all stood there motionless—until the hawk ruffled quickly, hunching its wings at its sides and tentatively at first, and then suddenly, all at once, teetered, righted itself on one claw, and then stepped off onto Clara's arm. It was heavier than she first thought, and her arm dipped before she compensated for the extra weight. Comfortable, and then looking to see that the hawk seemed steady as well, she backed away from the cage and pulled her arm, and the hawk, out into the open.

"Oh shit!" Mara had her hands over both ears and was gaping at her sister. "Oh man, be careful, huh? Damn ..."

Standing there with the bird standing on her, Clara entered a dream world where time slowed, and she began buzzing inside. Her ears were filled with the sound of blood pumping through her heart, and her nose filled with the scent of the hawk, resembling nothing so much as how she remembered quilts smelling as they were being taken from a cedar cabinet on the dawn of winter.

"Here you go," Clara walked over and let the hawk step off onto a picnic table nearest the rear door. "Hold still, and I'll get that." She then sat down at the table and very carefully, with both hands, began to untie the end of the tether around one of the hawk's clawed feet. Pulling off the leather band, she turned to Mara. "Okay, I think we're ready."

Mara stood as if hypnotized before realizing that both Clara and the hawk were looking at her. "Oh. Oh yeah," she stammered, snapping out of it, "... yeah, the door. I got it."

Clara turned back to the hawk. With it standing in front of her on the table, she placed both hands lightly on it sides, almost cupping the bird in her grasp. She could feel its heart beating in her fingers. She leaned in close.

"I'm going to stay here," she whispered, "and finish this." With tears in her eyes she smiled at the hawk. "But a part of me will continue on with you. Forever."

Pulling her hands away, Clara leaned back. For a moment she and the hawk sat there looking at one another, before finally the bird twitched and fluttered out its wings, at which point Mara's gasp reached Clara's ears. It then turned and dropped over the edge of the table, took flight and sailed out the open door into the night sky.

*   *   *

Officer Nelson Little had seen a lot of things in his years on the force. He could now add to that a lot of things he'd seen in the early-morning hour or so he'd just spent standing watch on the boardwalk along the edge of an ocean. A most immodestly dressed crowd of young girls had brought a rush of blood to his head with their equally immodest proposal; a military man, in full camouflaged fatigues, dried something-or-other all down the front of him, stopped to salute before walking off sideways; a crazy-looking old hippie couple called him a fascist pig and ran off. It just didn't stop, one after another, each more fascinating than the last. Watching the two women stroll by looking at him, the one eating a Polish ice and the other blowing him a kiss, he was thinking that he could have stood there all night when it suddenly dawned on him.

"Hey!" he called after them, hitching up his belt and running across the boardwalk. "Wait for me!"

Life. It begins with that, and then the rest of your days begin falling into place. You wear it like a cape and do what it is you do, all the while never really being able to put completely out of mind the fact that you're getting old and gray and wide—stooped, sore, and fragile. It's all so … unfeasible. It was always going to happen. It's just that it happened so fast: squinting to read the new prescription bottle instructions, the blood on your toothbrush, and the hair around the shower drain.

Did you find the time? Did you get it all in? The clock really is ticking.

Love. It begins with that, and then the rest of your life begins falling into place. Don't listen to anyone who tells you otherwise: it's worth the chance. If you are lucky, you are surrounded by people who love you. And even if you are not, you love someone. Admit it—even if only to yourself. Maybe it is wrong, on all fronts, doomed to fail with no future. If that's the case, then there's nothing to lose. What's the worst that's going to happen? Twenty-four years down the road you'll close your eyes and remember them, and how they made you feel, and you'll smile?

Find the time. Get it in. Really. The clock is ticking.

She let the phone ring and ring and ring. Long past the point where if there'd been anyone there they would have picked it up, she let it ring—the intermittent bell tone coming back to her like some second hand counting off the time from a life that seemed increasingly far away and long ago. She knew that ring, recognized it immediately and, with that, traveled all the way down the line and was there now, in each pulse, looking around at all that she'd fled from: the lumpy wallpaper in the different bedrooms, the mismatched kitchen appliances, and scuff marks that wouldn't wipe off hallway walls. Ring. The blue light seeping out from under the closed home office door, and standing on the roof naked.

Yeah, she thought, hanging up the motel-lobby payphone. *That rings a bell.*

Across the lobby, she could see that the desk clerk and the room maid were setting out baskets of fresh fruit and sweet buns next to large decanters of brewing coffee—standard motel continental breakfast fare on a folding table for paying guests in the morning. It looked and smelled divine. Clara walked out front and put a cigarette into her watering mouth, biding time until she could take a tray back to the room.

The sun was only just beginning to crest the ocean behind her. From where she stood under the motel veranda, she could look down the boulevard and see that most of the neon signs were still lit and glowing in the purple light. She would remember those 'vacancy' signs long from now, signaling to her that she was welcome at a time when she needed a place to belong. A flock of gulls swirled overhead, nosily making their way out to the seaside, and for a moment she took wing with them, looking up into the increasingly azure sky.

Somewhere up there, she thought to herself, tingling at the memory never to be forgotten.

From a long way off she watched as the station wagon made its way down the boulevard toward her, slowing in front of each motel and then continuing on to the next. Clara stood smoking and watched its halting progress, when it finally came alongside, slowed, and the driver pulled up and under the veranda where she was standing. Out of state tags—way out of state tags. *That must have been one hell of a drive*, she was thinking when the driver, leaving the engine running, parked it and stepped out the door. With two sleeping children buckled into the backseat, in front of what looked like enough suitcases to cover a trip around the whole country, and their apparent father sawing a log up front on the passenger side, the no-nonsense-looking woman with the cat-eye glasses and the bouffant-hairdo smoothed down her sundress with both hands before walking over to where Clara was standing.

She drew back and looked Clara over carefully first. "Excuse me," she decided to say. "Is this a nice motel, a safe place to stay?"

Clara took one last drag on her cigarette before exhaling and flicking it toward the sand bucket next to the entrance. They both watched as it dropped right in. The driver turned back to her.

"Yes, very much," said Clara. "It's been a life-saver."

The driver considered this for a moment, looking directly at Clara, before finally nodding and walking over to the station wagon. Reaching in through the open passenger-side window she placed a hand flat on her husband's chest and thoroughly shook him awake. "Wake up," she informed him. "We're here."

*　*　*

"One day …," chewing and chewing and chewing, breathing through her nose.

"What?" Clara, sitting crossed legged on her bed, looked over to where Mara was lying back into a pile of pillows on hers, and laying into a croissant roll she'd accessorized with help from the stairwell vending machine.

"I said," she said, washing it down with carbonated fruit punch, "that one day you are going to tell me what this was all about, right?"

Clara played with her food, swirled the paper cup full of milk and corn flakes around in her hand, and … wanted to. She looked over at her sister. For a while longer the two of them continued to eat breakfast in silence, looking at one another off and on while sorting and picking through the two-of-every-thing tray. Satisfied, Clara poured what milk she had left in her carton into the tall paper cup of coffee, opened the door to the room, looking up and down the second-floor exterior walkway first before lighting a cigarette and standing in the frame. She turned and looked back at Mara while blowing the smoke out the corner of her mouth. She didn't say anything, simply nodded her head up and down slightly. Mara in turn returned the gesture, smiling with half her mouth.

Clara turned in on herself and stared, methodically smoking while looking at her sister without inference. Mara sat looking at her, before abruptly throwing the covers on her bed aside and turning away. *Oh no*, Clara thought, on seeing that her sister was shielding her eyes. She flicked her cigarette over the railing and pulled the door shut behind her, leaning back against it to face into the room.

"Goddamn it," Mara sniffed with her back still to her. "It's me, huh, me," and she turned, got on her feet, and came up fast.

Pained, seeing right through her sister and into what she suspected she knew, Mara blocked any exist and held her in place with her eyes. "I don't know what's going on here, everything. I know that. But what I do know is," and she put a finger into Clara's vision, "you're not going to leave me behind again. No more 'alone and forgotten.' And you have to try, okay? For us. You got it?"

Clara was at once simultaneously conflicted, in full agreement and more than a little relieved.

"I don't know your kid," Mara was saying. "But given time they come around. I've seen that enough. He's yours, which means he's ours. That'll count for something eventually. He'll see that. As for your asshole husband, well," she threw her head back as if spitting him out, "he can go fuck himself as far as I'm concerned, even if that's part of what brought all this on to begin with, I guess ..." She dismissed him out of hand with a wave of hers.

"But for you," turning back to Clara. "You owe yourself another chance to make it work, okay? Is that what you've been waiting to hear? Don't just throw it all away without a fight. Go home, spell it out, punch it up a little, and let the bastard have it. That's your life too. You're worth it, and if that prick can't figure that out, screw him." Mara stood there adamant with her hands on her hips. "Worst case scenario? Pack your bag and come home. We'll never look back, okay?"

Clara was vibrating when she thought, *Really?*

"Of course," Mara said out loud, reading her mind. "And do you know why?" Clara was shaking her head no when Mara reached out and placed her hand over Clara's heart. "Because," she leaned in and whispered, "I was here first."

Sparkling in the sunlight and thundering up onto the sand, one after another, the morning tides arrived. Tremendous waves leeched out the last vestiges of the storm, diffusing the energy in a futile effort at reclamation: the end of the road would not be easily surrendered. Littering the surf as if a reminder that the hope in a future beyond will not easily be submerged, a million white plastic dish drainers mocked the natural order in a suggestion of the perseverance of uselessness. It isn't going to matter what we suspect to be true. We're dreamers, and we'll build a reef out of petroleum-based byproducts and tell ourselves that life persists. The eye of the beholder sees from the heart.

*   *   *

"Look at that guy out there." She was looking out from between the motel room curtains toward the surf. "What a goofball." Mara was rocking left and right on her feet while holding the curtain open with both hands. Letting go, she looked back toward where Clara was sitting on the edge of the bed. "What are we going to do with him, huh?"

Clara sat and looked at her sister standing there in her cheap bathing suit, a motel towel wrapped around her waist, new wide-brimmed wicker hat, and wearing sunglasses. "What do you mean?"

"I mean," Mara said, turning back to the window, "is he good for us? Should we keep him around when we get back home?"

Clara smiled at Mara's back. "I think," and she softened her tone, "you know the answer to that already." And before Mara could have her turn to ask, "What do you mean?", Clara went ahead and answered the question herself.

"Okay, I'll go home and deal with whatever I have to," she said. "But when I come back to see you, no matter what happens with me, I'll be looking to come back and see him as well. Is he good for us? Are we good for him? I don't know. But," she declared, "it has been good."

That brought Mara around. "Hey," she asked, "it has, hasn't it?"

"Are you up to it?" Clara asked, purposely prodding her from behind.

"You're right," Mara declared, clicking her tongue and turning back around. "It's all very exhausting—it's a lot of work being me. But this," and she resumed looking through the curtain, "this I got." She started laughing, quietly at first, and then in a sudden burst, "Hey!" she held the curtains and almost swung around to look at Clara again. "I'm going to run out there, sneak up, and push him in the water. Ha!" Her wide smile mixed deviousness and pure euphoria in equal measure.

"Why on earth?" Clara questioned with hands out, smiling back. Mara laughed and ducked out the door.

Time.

She knew it was.

She'd reclaimed everything but that, and that would not wait forever. She was past the middle of her life and felt renewed; surrounded by love. It was as if, suddenly the ticking had stopped. A silent alarm sounded, and she almost jumped, standing there in her shorts in the middle of the bathroom floor. Time. The green tiles cooled her under the florescent light, looking across the sink at her own reflection. From a distance, no hesitation was visible, no fear.

Take a deep breath.

And go.

She could hear the overhead ultraviolet light buzzing in the glass tube. She could taste the moisture seeping in from the sea. She closed her eyes, held her arms out in front of her, splayed her fingers apart, and could feel the air-conditioning floating around her hands.

Magnification washed over her.

Stepping up to the sink, she leaned in to the mirror, zeroing in on her own eyes as closely as she could without losing focus. Holding the basin with one hand, she was breathing deep and long—pronounced bouts of air being forced in and out as fast as she could, as if stealing breath. She pressed her hand flat against her belly and slid up and under her breast, letting her fingers slide across.

There was nothing she wouldn't have done to have experienced the last couple of weeks, to have had the time.

There was nothing she wouldn't have done, to have been with them and to see all of those people again.

There was nothing.

She was weeping when her legs buckled, and she slowly collapsed onto the porcelain sink in front of her, her skin squeaking off it, and then sliding down onto her knees, thumping the tile floor hard, palms out leaning forward and tears streaming straight down.

She did this herself, alone, was here in the flesh. And she saw all this transpire from somewhere else—the eye of the beholder sees from the heart.

*   *   *

Clara Kozlowski stood with both hands on the railing outside her motel room and looked across the beach at Officer Nelson Little. The policeman, looking anything but in his new vacation getup, was standing alone at the water's edge and facing out toward the sea. All around, waves were depositing, between more tangled racks of kitchen utensils, piles of yellow and pink jellyfish like great translucent plastic trash bags sloshing up onto the beach, only to then drag the entire discombobulation back out into the surf. The silver storage containers, sporadically dotting the length of the beach in each direction as far as the eye could see, only added to the surrealism of the entirety.

The appropriateness of it all wasn't lost on Clara.

She was nearly swooning under the morning sunlight when she heard her name on the air. Her grip on the rail tightened as she watched him waving both arms over his head, looking across at her now, his mouth open, and his words mingling with the crashing surf. Straining to hear, she was squinting at his mouth trying to make out what was being said, and she almost missed her, Mara breaking out of a strand of tall grass along a dune off to one side and running across the beach.

Oh god, Clara's thoughts welled up through a sense of shared adrenaline as she watched her sister speeding unseen across the sand, her sheer unchecked joy visible like a halo even from a distance.

Rising on the balls of her feet, nearly shuddering, she was listening to the wind, straining and listening to hear Nelson's declaration:

"It's all so … *fabulous!*"

He was shouting, throwing his arms straight up, just before Mara crashed into him from behind and sent him toppling into the waves.

"Yes!" yelled Clara, seeing but not hearing her sister's laughter.

Yes, it is.

ACKNOWLEDGMENTS

The author would like to thank several people who provided support and inspiration along the way: Pam, whose enthusiasm early on inspired a confidence that carried through to completion; Valerie (with a keen eye) and John (with a good heart); Deb, who lives her life her way in her sister's heart; an anonymous neighbor penciling in stark truths; and the Ramones, for acceleration.

Printed in the United States
By Bookmasters